Three Day Summer

Three Day Summer

Sarvenaz Tash

SIMON & SCHUSTER BFYR

NEW YORK   LONDON   TORONTO   SYDNEY   NEW DELHI

SIMON & SCHUSTER BFYR

An imprint of Simon & Schuster Children's Publishing Division
1230 Avenue of the Americas, New York, New York 10020

SIMON & SCHUSTER BFYR is a trademark of Simon & Schuster, Inc.
For information about special discounts for bulk purchases, please contact Simon &
Schuster Special Sales at 1-866-506-1949 or business@simonandschuster.com.
The Simon & Schuster Speakers Bureau can bring authors to your live event. For more
information or to book an event, contact the Simon & Schuster Speakers Bureau at
1-866-248-3049 or visit our website at www.simonspeakers.com.
Book design by Krista Vossen
The text for this book is set in Bembo.
Manufactured in the United States of America
2 4 6 8 10 9 7 5 3 1
Library of Congress Cataloging-in-Publication Data
Tash, Sarvenaz.
Three day summer / Sarvenaz Tash. — 1st edition.
pages cm
Summary: During the three days of the music festival known as Woodstock,
Michael Michaelson of Somerville, Massachusetts, and Cora Fletcher, a volunteer in
the medical tent who lives nearby, share incredible experiences, the greatest of which is
meeting each other.
ISBN 978-1-4814-3931-2 (hardcover) — ISBN 978-1-4814-3933-6 (eBook)
[1. Woodstock Festival (1969 : Bethel, N.Y.)—Fiction. 2. Music festivals—Fiction. 3. Love—
Fiction. 4. Counterculture—Fiction. 5. Nineteen sixties—Fiction. 6. Woodstock (N.Y.)—
History—20th century—Fiction.] I. Title.
PZ7.T2111324Thr 2015
[Fic]—dc23
2014032737

To Graig—
for all the summers of love
(and winters, falls, and springs, too)

Three Day Summer

Thursday, August 14

chapter 1
Cora

"You. Are. A. Candy. Cane."

The boy grips me by the arms, his enormous glassy eyes staring right at my chest through his long bangs.

Under normal circumstances, I would feel terrified and violated. Instead, I roll my eyes.

"He means candy striper," Anna says as she zips across the tent, bringing paper cups of water to the zoned-out patients slumped against the far side.

"Yeah, I get it," I say before calmly extracting the boy's fingers from my arms. "Sir," I say as firmly as I can. "Have a seat."

Of course, there are no available chairs to sit on, but the ground is probably a sea of fluffy marshmallows to this guy. At least, based on the way he momentarily forgets he has knees and goes crashing to the floor.

"He'll feel that in the morning," Anna says as she zips back.

"He's not feeling it now," I mutter as the boy stares at the hem of my dress with a goofy grin plastered on his face. He's drooling.

"Mmmmm . . . candy."

It's only eleven a.m. on Thursday. The concert hasn't even started yet.

It's going to be a very long weekend.

chapter 2
Michael

"We need to be there, Michael. Have you seen this lineup? It's going to be *the* event of the year. Maybe even the decade." Amanda had been flushed with excitement when she'd shown me the newspaper ad a month ago.

The thing was that I agreed with her. At the time, I was just too pissed off at her to let her know that. She'd thrown a fit in front of my friends just the night before, getting hysterical because I'd casually said I didn't know how I felt about maybe getting drafted.

"How can you not know?" she'd screamed. "They are going to drag you into a swamp and make you kill people all in the twisted name of capitalism. Your apathy is the problem, Michael." Then she'd stalked off, expecting me to follow.

Which, of course, I had. Not without a few choice words from my friends. "Make sure you get your pecker back from her purse, dude," was the one ringing in my ear the loudest by the time I reached her.

Standing by my mom's car, Amanda had berated me again before dissolving into tears at the thought that she cared more about my life than I did. Unfortunately, Amanda was beautiful when she cried, especially in that moment, with the teardrops clinging to the curve of her cheek, glittering with the reflection of starlight. Before I knew it, I was kissing her and apologizing, telling her that it was going to be okay.

But in the glare of daylight, I was annoyed that I'd let her spew some nonsense I wasn't even sure she believed in—she'd probably just been rummaging for an excuse to make me chase after her. And I'd given in to her drama.

I didn't want to do it again, especially as she'd clutched the festival ad and said dramatically, "And if you don't take me, we are over. Once and for all." She'd turned to another Amanda standby: the puffed-out lips move.

Yes! That's what I wanted. To be over. Only . . . every time I got up the nerve to try to tell her that, I'd catch a glimpse of her blueberry-colored eyes or the way her soft, tanned skin peeked through something she was wearing and then we'd be kissing and . . . I couldn't do it. In fact, I was pretty sure I'd never be able to. Let's face it, blaming my pecker was not entirely inaccurate.

But then she'd actually shown me the lineup for this festival. Jefferson Airplane, Canned Heat, the Grateful Dead, and Jimi freaking Hendrix on one bill? 3 DAYS OF PEACE & MUSIC, the ad promised. Three whole days. Not to mention it was all happening less than two hundred miles away from us.

I looked at Amanda's big blue eyes and the flower she'd drawn on her perfect face. She knew these bands almost as well as I did; she knew what having them all in one place would mean. And I thought, maybe this would be an ideal reason not to want to break up. Maybe we would go and bond over all that glorious music, like we had in the beginning, and I'd realize that the inside of Amanda matched the outside after all, and, for the love of all that is holy, we would finally do it.

Which is how I find myself driving my mom's purple Chrysler Crown Imperial, Amanda in the front seat, her friends Suzie and Catherine giggling in the back with my friend Evan. The car is a boat, which is why the large-and-in-charge Evan can fit back there with two other people. At six foot five and with 1) the charm and sense of humor of a Smothers Brother and 2) a seemingly bottomless stash of hash at his disposal, Evan is popular with everybody. But especially the ladies.

It's like two different worlds happening in the front and back of the car. A full-out riotous party in the rear and all the tension of the Cuban missile crisis up where I am.

Amanda is complaining about how hot it is. She's been doing so for the past hour, during which we've been crawling along Route 17B. I keep looking nervously at the hood, waiting for smoke to come billowing out. It wouldn't be the first time it's overheated. Something Amanda also knows and keeps repeating.

A sharp rap at my window makes me turn. A state trooper

stands there. I can see my own (thankfully) sober green eyes in his reflective glasses. From my peripheral vision, I quickly glimpse Evan stashing something in his pocket. Only then do I roll down the window.

"You kids here for the festival?" the cop asks in a friendly tone.

"Yes, sir," I say. I can feel Amanda rolling her eyes behind me. She hates anything that indicates we are bowing down to "the man," which, among other things includes her father, cops, teachers, and, for some reason, Dick Clark. She has a weird theory about him rigging the music scene in the fifties, which she says is anti-democracy or something.

"Well, we are suggesting that everyone turn back," the cop continues. "There won't be enough room on the festival site to accommodate everybody, and this traffic isn't going anywhere. Please turn around the next chance you get." The cop nods and doesn't wait for my response before sauntering away.

There's silence in the car for a moment. "What do we do?" Suzie says from the backseat.

"We keep going, obviously," Amanda says in exasperation. "Of course the state trooper wants all of us to turn back. Look at us. We're the blue meanies' worst nightmare." She indicates the sea of cars around us, which includes more than one psychedelically painted van. "I heard there's plenty of room at the site. And we can't *not* be there."

Damn it. It's so infuriating that her words are actually logical, when the way she says them makes me want to tongue an exhaust pipe.

We stay in the car, of course. But only for about another thirty minutes. The Chrysler finally overheats and I'm forced to pull it over onto the grass by the side of the road. We get out and I open the hood, not that I know much about what I can do to fix it. I try not to look at Amanda. I think I can only deal with one steaming entity at a time.

In the meantime, Evan gets out and walks over to a nearby car to talk to its passenger.

"All right," he says when he gets back. "I think we're less than five miles from the site. We can walk it, right?" He turns and grins at Amanda and the girls. I sneak a peek at them too, hoping Evan has managed to defuse the situation. As usual, he has.

"Sure," Suzie says cheerfully, and the rest of the girls nod along.

I take one final look at the car and send up a quick prayer that nothing will happen to my mom's pride and joy. Then I grab my backpack, Catherine her sleeping bag, and Evan his Riveting Rucksack of Good Times, as he calls it. We're not the only people who have pulled over, it seems, so we follow a small line of people cheerfully walking their way to *the* concert of the year.

chapter 3
Cora

At twelve thirty, I'm due for a break, so I slip out of the medical tent and walk the mile and a half to my house. It's weird to see people lounging around the normally empty field I take to get there.

It's even weirder when I approach my big gray farmhouse to see the skinny, bespectacled boy emerging from it. I swear my heart changes its rhythm then, beating *Ned, Ned, Ned* over and over again. I swallow something acrid.

He waves at me and walks over. "How is it down there?" he asks casually.

Of course he's casual. It can't possibly hurt that much to be the heartbreaker as opposed to the heartbroken. No matter what he said in his little speech last month.

Oh, God, it's been over a month. I feel pathetic.

In a semblance of calm, I carefully untie my candy striper apron and take it off.

"Okay," I say, willing my voice to stay steady. "It's already getting crowded."

"Damn hippies!" Ned intones in a pretty spot-on imitation of my dad before breaking into laughter.

I smile weakly. He doesn't get to make fun of my dad anymore, does he?

"I'm definitely going to go check it out later," he says, "so maybe I'll see you around."

"Yeah, maybe," I murmur. Though really, I hope not. I think it's going to be hard enough working the medical tent without Ned's stupid smile distracting me.

I watch him brush off a spot of dirt from his hand. Even though I know he's just gotten off a shift plowing my dad's farm, his hands are impeccably clean. Mom is always happy to let him clean up before he leaves, impressed by his dedication to personal hygiene. I wonder where her loyalties lie.

"Later," he says, giving me that ridiculous smile before strolling away down the road to his own house.

I love-hate him so much.

Bastard.

When I walk through the front door, the smell of Ivory soap is still wafting around the hallway bathroom. I peek in, for a moment picturing Ned covered in suds up to his elbows.

"Cora, could you grab the eggs?" Mom's head appears from the kitchen, a mass of wavy dark hair. Thanks to my grandmother, we have the same coppery skin tone, the same sharp cheekbones, and the same color hair, only hers is thick and wavy and mine is straight, fine, and currently brushing my waistline.

I turn away from the traitorous hallucination in the bathroom to my mom. "It's Wes's turn," I say.

Mom sighs. "I know. He's gone, though."

I let out a disgruntled groan but then walk through the house and to the backyard door to grab the basket. My twin brother is getting scarcer by the day.

"Oh!" my mom calls excitedly. "Mark wrote. I left your letter on the dining room table."

Instant smile. Suddenly I don't mind the walk in the sunshine to the henhouse. I think of my eventual reward as I methodically gather the smooth and speckled eggs while eighty hens lose their ever-loving minds around me. They aren't the brightest, the hens, but I still love them. I pretend they recognize me when I walk in, even though I'm pretty sure they wake up every morning surprised to find they are, in fact, chickens.

"Hullo there, twenty-three," I greet a particularly plump one, who screeches at me, I like to think, in welcome. I say the number 23 in French, though: *vingt-trois*. My dad never lets us name the animals on the farm, saying we'll get too attached when the time comes to bring them to the table. But the French numbers make them seem a little less impersonal somehow, and just a tad more elegant.

I savor the anticipation of my older brother's letter. He's

stationed in Vietnam, and hearing from him is more rare than I would like. But whenever I do, it's like a small weight has been lifted off my heart, one that slowly starts pressing its way down again as soon as I've read a letter.

Hearing from him means he is still alive.

There are always three letters in every one of his envelopes. One for my parents, one for Wes, and one for me. In one of his first letters to me two years ago, he told me as a joke to grow out my hair in protest of the war. I took it to heart.

I smile as my hair creates a dark curtain every time I bend down to gather another egg, and wonder what his letter will say this time. He always includes funny anecdotes about the other soldiers and sometimes even himself. I blushed a little last time when he mentioned the "house of ill repute" they'd managed to swing by while stationed in Hanoi. I wonder if his buddy Jack found his army-issued underwear in time before the house got raided. Mark ended the letter on a cliff-hanger.

I pluck the last egg from No. 80's (*quatre-vingts'*) nest and practically skip into the house, eager for a conversation with my older brother. Even if it's one-sided.

chapter 4
Michael

"Bethel" sounds like a girl's name. A sweet, maybe plain sort of girl you can take home to your parents.

I can see the town lives up to that sentiment. It's nice and neat, acres and acres of squared-off farmland, dotted with white clapboard houses here and there. The particular saturated green of August provides a contrast to the unkempt, colorful tide of humanity that is now steadily flowing through it.

"Evan!" a voice calls out.

We turn around to see a black kid with overgrown hair, unbuttoned shirt, and red-striped bell-bottoms striding over to us. He's wearing large white-framed sunglasses. "I thought it was you, man," he says as he claps Evan on the shoulder.

"Hey, Rob. How are you?" Evan grins.

"About to witness an amazing show, man. How do you think?" Rob says good-naturedly.

"You said it," Evan says.

"I'm actually really glad I ran into you. My girl and her friends aren't supposed to get in until tomorrow. Mind if I hang with your crew until then?" He looks over at us. I can already see both Suzie and Catherine eyeing him moonily. I guess he's pretty good-looking.

"Not at all. *Nos casa* is *su casa*," Evan says before introducing us all. Even Amanda bestows one of her dazzling smiles on Rob. The same smile that practically stopped my heart the first time I saw it across the record store aisle.

But since the car ride hasn't made me feel too optimistic about this weekend solving all our problems, I suddenly get hit with a little jolt of inspiration: What if somehow Amanda cheats on me with Rob and then I can finally use that as an excellent excuse to end it? I start to walk a little behind them, so that maybe they'll have more of a chance to talk. Just in case.

The nice thing about arriving on Thursday, a full day before the show is set to start, is that we have a good pick of where to camp out.

Or at least, that's what I thought.

"Evan, man, you got the tickets?" I ask as I see some metal gates in the distance.

"Sure, man," Evan says with a laugh. "We are the tickets." He stops and does a little twirl, finishing with a hand flourish that air-presents the length of this body.

"What?" I'm not really getting Evan's joke. When I first mentioned the festival a month ago to Evan, he said he would take care of getting us in if I could take care of getting us there. Obviously, I have fulfilled my end of the bargain.

"It's gonna be a free festival, man, don't worry about it."

"No, it's not," says Amanda before turning to me. "Is this because you were too cheap to give him the eighteen bucks?"

I roll my eyes. "No, Miss A," I say. "Evan, what did you do with my thirty-six dollars then?" Chivalrous (read: stupid) boyfriend that I am, I've already fronted the money for both Amanda and me for all three days. Amanda has this annoying habit of getting all feminist and ranty on me when I open doors for her but then becoming all wide-eyed with batty eyelashes when it comes to picking up the tab.

Evan grins. "Don't worry, man. It's all in here," he says as he pats his backpack, which makes a dull, satisfied sound. "I have everything you need to make this an experience you won't ever forget for the rest of your life. One that will make paltry thirty-six your favorite number in the whole word."

Drugs. He's spent my money on drugs. Normally, I wouldn't care because he always shares and it seems to work out in the end. But this time, we won't be able to get *into* the concert. And we're stuck in the middle of Podunk, USA. Not to mention Amanda is going to cut my balls off, draw a flower on them, and save them as a souvenir.

But just as she screws up her face and opens her mouth to yell, Rob cuts in. "My cat's right, man. I've heard there's a million people coming. No way they're going to be able to keep all those people outside. Those fences are coming down. Trust me."

Evan nods emphatically. "In the meantime," he says, "let's check out the luxurious accommodations that Bethel has to offer. Miss A and the Mandettes are sure to dig it." Evan's nickname for Amanda and her two friends. They love it, of course. Nobody seems to notice that when I call Amanda Miss A, it's with a sneer.

We continue to walk to Evan's "luxurious accommodations," which turn out to be a field outside the fences. Now that we're closer to them, I can see that the gates aren't even fully erected yet. A couple of people appear to be slowly fiddling with some tools down one end. Down the other, a lone guy in a red shirt seems to be the only sort of official-looking person even manning them. Meanwhile, the field is already dotted with reposing kids. I start to relax.

"If we don't get in, because of *your* friend, Michael," Amanda hisses at me underneath a perfect smile. "I will kill you."

Great. Death by Woodstock. Well, I hope it happens *after* Hendrix plays.

chapter 5
Cora

DON'T BUY YASGUR'S MILK! HE LOVES HIPPIES! The sign is huge, the letters almost taller than me and I stand about five foot four. If a sign could scream, this one would be out of lung capacity.

But that's not what makes me stop in my tracks as I'm walking across the little field to my shift in the medical tent. No, I screech to a halt because of the five-foot-six sweaty farmer who's emphatically hammering the sign's left post into the ground with his good arm.

"Dad?" I say in disbelief.

My father looks up at me, his eyes squinting into the sun. I'm wearing my candy striper apron again and a plain blue dress underneath it. None of that "hippie nonsense," as my dad is fond of calling some of my friends' more fashionable duds. Not that it seems to matter anyway because the glint of disappointment is suddenly diamond bright in his eyes.

"And where do you think you're going, young lady?" he asks.

It takes everything I have not to roll my eyes. I sigh. "Dad, I'm working the medical tents. You know that."

"Damn hippies. If they're going to get themselves liquored up and drugged up and God knows *what else*, they don't need *my* daughter's help to get them back on the straight and narrow. They can sleep it off like everybody else."

I point at the sign. "Mr. Yasgur, Dad? Really?" Max Yasgur owns more land than anyone in all of Sullivan County. He's the purveyor of most of our milk and a sweet, soft-spoken guy. As of about three weeks ago, he also happens to own the farm that's about to host an enormous music festival. No surprise that my dad and some of Bethel's other disgruntled citizens have done everything in their power to try to stop him from leasing it. The idea of rock stars, and hippies, and fifty thousand young people descending upon our sleepy little farm town is not exactly a palatable idea to people like Dad.

Obviously, their protests haven't been working. But asking people to boycott Mr. Yasgur's milk? This is just too much.

"This is what he gets," my dad says stubbornly. "We told him it'd be like this and we're as good as our word."

"It's just a music festival, Dad. Jeez, what do you think is going to happen?"

Oh, crud. Now I've done it. Dad's face has just become six shades of red, his cheeks and the tip of his nose flaming as brightly as a siren.

"Cora Fletcher. I wonder if that's exactly what some seventeen-year-old girl said to her dad right before the Democratic convention. Right before she got her head bashed in at the riot. Or how about before Martin Luther King was assassinated? Or what about President Kennedy?! Just a parade on Main Street?! Is that what that was?"

"Dad, there are no presidents or dignitaries here. It's just a rock show," I mutter.

"This music gets all you kids riled up and then you're all *tumbling* and who knows what your brain is telling the rest of you to do."

He means "tripping," not "tumbling," but this doesn't seem like the right time to get into semantics.

"Okay, Dad. Okay. Just calm down, all right?" He had a mild heart attack just a year ago and I don't need him to have another one. "I'm just going to be working the medical tent with Anna. That's all. Everything will be fine."

Anna is the nurse I usually volunteer under. She recruited me two weeks ago for this—basically as soon as we all found out that the festival was kicked out of Wallkill, New York, and about to suddenly descend on Bethel instead. (Funnily enough, I don't think it was ever slated to take place in the actual town of Woodstock.) Anna is also a friend of the family. I can see Dad's red cheeks fade into a slightly less alarming dark pink.

This is my cue to skedaddle. "See you later, Dad," I say quickly as I turn around and practically flee across the field, nearly going face-first into something dark and sculpted. Wait a minute, those are pecs.

I let my eyes follow the chest muscles up to a grinning face, dazzling teeth matching bright white sunglasses. "What's the rush, sister?"

"Ergh" or some hideous noise close to that comes out of my mouth.

He takes my hand and gives it a loose shake. "I'm Rob."

Rob is beautiful. He's also wearing an unbuttoned denim shirt and tight striped pants that showcase how beautiful *all* of him really is.

"See you around," he says before ambling off. He's with three girls and two other guys. One of the girls is tall and blond, wearing a long, rainbow-colored dress and silver rings on each of her ten fingers, a dainty daisy drawn on her cheek. The other two are darker, one dressed in tiny denim shorts and a midriff-baring crocheted vest, the other wearing a shorter dress that's dripping with beaded turquoise necklaces. The two boys are both in bell-bottoms, one about the same height as Rob and carrying a humongous backpack and the other slightly shorter and skinnier with longish dirty blond hair and something that looks like the palest wisps of peach fuzz around his lips.

The girls pay me no attention, and Rob and Backpack Guy have clearly already forgotten about my existence. But Peach Fuzz keeps his gaze on me a moment longer as they walk away, nearly walking into Rob, too.

Hmmm—I look down to assess myself—*pretty sure he was staring at my legs.* And then I remember I'm in my stupid uniform.

I roll my eyes at myself. Not exactly the height of fashion, especially compared to the company he's keeping. I shake my head and start walking—with purpose this time—back to Mr. Yasgur's farm.

chapter 6
Michael

That chick has nice legs.

Really nice. Sort of a glowing, deep golden color, tapering perfectly at the ankles and everything. She's wearing some sort of weird stripy uniform thing, though, which I vaguely remember as meaning something. Nun in training, maybe? I hope not. What a waste of legs.

By the time I peel my eyes away from her, Evan and the crew have plopped down on a bit of grass in the meadow and Evan is digging into his backpack.

He takes out a bunch of bananas, a thermos, four teal plastic cups, and a tin packed nearly to the brim with weed. He also takes out a small brass pipe, which he sets about packing.

Rob eyes the bananas. "Think we can go look for some real food after this? I wouldn't want anything as prehistoric as hunger pains to invade my consciousness once the music starts. Know what I mean?"

I nod emphatically as I take the pipe Evan is offering me. "Since we're not in yet anyway, maybe we should hit that lunch counter we passed on our way here? In that little town . . . White Lake?"

"Cool," Evan says as he repacks the bananas, thermos, and cups.

The pipe goes around once and then we get up and start ambling back. The town we passed on our way from my car is about three miles away, but I don't mind the walk. We don't have anywhere to be yet, it's a beautiful day, and the weed has created a nice buffer of calm, as per usual. Even Amanda is holding my hand and keeping the peace.

White Lake seems to have a sort of main street with a couple of shops, a grocery store, and the lunch counter I remembered. There is a small line out its glass door, but since we have nothing but time, we cheerfully get on the end of it.

"I'm not going back, Jane," a girl in front of me with braided red hair says to her friend.

"What are you gonna do if you're not in college, Meg?" Jane shoots back, her eyes big with worry.

Meg shrugs. "I'll be fine. There are plenty of things that don't need a college degree. Growing food, playing music, becoming a mural painter. Anything. That school's stifling me! And besides, it's not like I have to worry about getting drafted."

It's like someone has taken an oil drill and tapped straight into the biggest nerve in my body. I go crashing down from my small high, about to explode into a million pieces.

I can hear the fight with my mom, the one we've been having practically every day of the summer. Pieces of it have just been echoed, word for word, in front of me.

"I don't want to go, Ma. I'll be fine. There are plenty of things I can do that have nothing to do with college."

"Not if you're dead in a field you can't. It's the safest way to stay out of Vietnam, Michael."

I don't think I want to go to Vietnam. I'm not a fighter. And sure, if I go to the community college I reluctantly enrolled in, I won't be drafted. But I know for sure I don't want to go to school. I just can't imagine ending up like my dad. He spends ten hours a day at his office. I assume he talks to people there, because by the time he comes home, he has no words left for Ma or me.

The worst is looking into his eyes. It's like looking at a burnt-out wick, dark and purposeless. When I was younger, I used to sometimes stare at other people's eyes to see if I could recognize the same thing in them. Is that what it meant to be an adult? That was when I started really getting into music. I'd look at pictures of my rock heroes. John Lennon never looked like that. Neither did Jerry Garcia. Or Donovan. Or Jimi Hendrix.

I have no idea what or who I want to be, but I know for certain what and who I don't. And that's all I see when I think about going to college. A one-way ticket to future soullessness.

"Hey, are you checking that girl out?!"

A sharp voice brings me out of my unpleasant daydream. Amanda's.

I look at her in a daze, only then realizing that I've been staring at the redhead.

"What?"

"Asshole!" Amanda says as she punches my arm.

The redhead catches my eye and gives me a small, secret smile.

I shrug and smile back before turning away. No need to fan the flames of Amanda's psychoses.

It takes us another forty-five minutes to get a table. By the time our burgers arrive, Amanda still isn't talking to me.

But, man, will I remember that meal. A juicy, perfectly cooked slab of meat, doused with ketchup, and large, crunchy slices of sour pickle. Perfectly salted fries, crispy. A Coke.

My consciousness definitely feels ready for whatever's about to come next.

chapter 7
Cora

I'm afraid, Cora.

I think of Mark's letter. This is the first time that he has ever said those exact words to me.

His terror is terrifying. My fearless older brother who's been gone so long now. Almost two and a half years. What could have happened that would cause him to be scared now when he never has been before? Or is it just that he has never told me before? Does he think I'm getting old enough to handle the truth now?

"Cheer up!" a voice says to me, and I look up to see an older guy in a big cowboy hat and white jumpsuit grinning at me. He's missing several of his front teeth.

"Ready for the time of your life?" he asks.

I give him a small smile. Despite my worry, something about his easy joy is infectious.

"Hugh, I can't find the gruel." A girl with frizzy brown hair and a guy with a long beard come up to the jumpsuit guy. They are both festooned with red bandannas with a picture of a white flying pig silk-screened on them. The guy wears his around his arm, and the girl uses hers to pull back her hair.

Hugh looks at them thoughtfully for a minute. "Aha! It's in the back of Lisa's van," he finally says triumphantly.

He turns around to walk away and I see that the back of his suit has a large embroidered blue and red star design. Very patriotic.

"I'm worried we won't have enough food," the girl says as they walk toward some food tents that have been set up across the small woods from the medical tents. She glances nervously at the significant number of people already gathering in small herds. There are a lot more of them than there were this morning. If I had to guess, I'd say the number has at least quadrupled.

"Worry? Now, why would you go and do a silly thing like that for?" Hugh says cheerfully. "We can feed fifty thou a day easily. It'll all be groovy."

Their voices fade as I veer to the right and walk past the woods to my little yellow tent, Hugh's red, white, and blue emblem watermarking my thoughts.

I wonder what the American flag means to Mark now, whether he still shares Dad's enthusiasm for it. He's tired of fighting in its name, that much I know. *I want to come home, Cora. More than that, I want all of us to come home.*

He didn't even finish the story of Jack and his underwear. It's the saddest letter he has ever written me.

I eye the knots of people everywhere, a lot around Mark's age of twenty-two, a lot around mine. He should be here with them. If he hadn't signed up for the army when he was the eager-eyed, antsy nineteen-year-old I had last seen—gung ho to follow in his father's footsteps instead of continuing college—he would be.

I catch a glimpse of one small group that seems to have somehow procured a sheep. A guy with shoulder-length red hair, a long orange tunic, and white pants is lovingly petting it. He looks like a reverse flame. My eyebrows raise and I'm immediately worried for the animal, especially in the hands of city folk. I decide I can keep an eye on it from my medical tent.

"How's it going?"

I turn. Wes, my brother, is sitting cross-legged right outside my tent, his light brown wavy hair hanging down to his shoulders. Even though he's my twin, we hardly look alike at all. Aside from the curl in his hair, Wes has almost all of Dad's coloring and features, and I have almost all of Mom's. Wes and Mark look a lot more like they could be twins than we do.

"You left me with the hens," I protest.

"Couldn't deal with the Drip kissing Mom's ass today. It was destroying my morning." The Drip is Wes's nickname for Ned. To be fair, he never really liked him even when he was my boyfriend. But ever since he accidentally caught me red-eyed the night we broke up, he's been particularly furious with him. Wes has seen me cry maybe twice ever, and I've cried maybe a lifetime total of five times. It's usually not how my emotions work, unless something bomb-shelter levels of catastrophic has happened.

"We have a letter from Mark," I say.

Wes smiles. "Cool. I'll check it out later. For now, do you have a bandage?" He holds up his right palm, where a pretty sizable wound is bleeding.

"What happened?" I ask as I kneel down beside him.

"No big thing. Just a splinter." He gestures nonchalantly at the sign next to him. END THE WAR NOW it blares. It's mounted on what looks like possibly the most decrepit piece of wood I've ever seen.

"Wes!" I squeal. "You're going to need a tetanus shot."

His eyes flash a second of fear and then narrow. "Small price to pay to try and save the millions who are, I don't know, being *killed* over there," he says with an attempt at valiance.

I sigh. "You're preaching to the choir, you know," I say as I take his noninjured hand in mine and help him up.

I turn around without another word, and he follows me into the tent, grumbling a low apology.

Walking over to the table we've set up, I take out some bandages, cotton balls, alcohol, and a dark bottle of Mercurochrome. I take his hand and examine it.

"There's a little piece of wood still in there. I'm going to have to take it out."

Grabbing tweezers, I wipe some alcohol on it, and start digging around in Wes's hand as gently as I can. He winces.

Wes isn't so good with physical pain. My father, the two-war veteran, rides him about it all the time, constantly comparing him to the derring-do of Mark, especially when Wes starts talking about dodging selective service.

Threshold of pain aside, I can't say I exactly blame him. Being a girl, I don't have to put my name down for a draft when I turn eighteen, so I'm not faced with the high probability of being sent into a battlefield. Though I am faced with the heart-wrenching possibility of coming out an only child at the end of everything. I'm not sure which is worse.

"Ow!" he yells when I finally pull the piece of wood out. To be fair to him, it is a rather long piece.

He hisses when I rub Mercurochrome on his wound, staining his skin orange before I wrap it up in a bandage.

"Thanks," he mumbles as he steps back toward the entrance of the tent.

"Not so fast." I grab the sleeve of his green tie-dyed shirt. "Tetanus shot."

"Oh, come on! It was just a tiny splinter," he whines.

"Not based on the noises you were making," I say. Turning around, I spot the middle-aged brunette I'm looking for. "Anna," I yell over to her, not daring to leave my brother's side in case he attempts escape. It wouldn't be the first time. "Can you give this fool a tetanus shot?" I point a thumb at Wes.

Without any hesitation, Anna looks into one of the dozens of bins neatly stacked up on the side of the tent and emerges with a syringe wrapped in plastic. She rummages around in another bin and comes up with a vial of liquid.

I turn to Wes, noticing his wide-eyed look of fear. Time for a distraction. "So where are Adam, Laurie, and Peter?"

"Protesting."

"*Obviously*," I say with an eye-roll. "But where are they? And really, you and Dad are opposite sides of the same coin. What do you think is going to happen by protesting *here*?"

Wes turns to me with a glare. "Millions of people are going to be watching this weekend, Cora. We're protesting for them to *see*. To hear just what this generation wants. And it ain't war! OW!!" he howls. Anna has stuck him with the needle.

"All done," I say with a grin as Anna places another bandage on his arm.

"Were you trying to get me riled up just so I wouldn't feel that?" he spits.

"Well . . . yeah," I say.

"Oh. Well, thanks. I guess."

I shake my head. "You're welcome. Try not to get into any more trouble out there, okay?"

Wes grins and, for a moment, his face sheds its conscientious-citizen mask and shows the unbridled excitement of a seventeen-year-old boy. "I can't believe this is happening in our own backyard. Can you?"

He practically skips out of the tent, carrying his sign in his unbandaged hand.

If nothing else, he'll definitely be getting another splinter.

chapter 8
Michael

Once the sun starts to set, I realize how wrong I've been about Bethel being a plain sort of girl. All her hidden beauties just come out later in the day. As we leave the lunch counter, the sky starts to streak pink and violet and orange. The colors are as unbelievable as a psychedelic concert poster and the entire scene is made kaleidoscopic by the reflection in the town's great big lake. Far out.

By the time we're back by the festival site, the stars have come out. More stars than I'd have ever known existed back in Boston. It's like someone is poking holes in a piece of sapphire paper and they have no sense of moderation. I wonder if this hypothetical person has any relation to Evan.

Speaking of which, our resident comedian has been amusing us by narrating the thoughts of the other kids we see heading toward what we've already come to feel is "our" field.

"Your cantaloupes are as supple as your tits," Evan says as one guy in a fringed vest stares freely at a braless girl in a thin shirt walking with a shopping bag of food, the rough green skin of a cantaloupe peeking out from the top. The girls scream in laughter.

"Evan, man, you get away with murder," Rob says with a chuckle.

"Tell me about it," I respond.

Soon, we've staked a claim to a corner of the field. There are two sleeping bags and six of us but, somehow, it seems to work out fine. Either Catherine or Suzie (or both) is in Evan's sleeping bag, while Rob is lying on a blanket. Things keep shifting over there, though, and there are plenty of giggles, so I have no idea how they end up.

Amanda is with me in my sleeping bag, sprawled out across my chest. Despite everything, I can't deny that she's nice to hold on to, warm and soft. Her hair is tickling my bare chest, its blond strands practically glowing by starlight. I bend down and kiss a piece of it.

I hear her laugh slightly and then sigh in contentment.

I look down at her profile. She's just so damn beautiful. I'm crazy to want to end things. Maybe it can always be like this: peaceful and perfect. Waiting on a tomorrow that is going to fuel everything that is wonderful about being young. I think again of the first time we met, that cold day in January, with the smell of dusty plastic in the air as I flipped through some older LPs—the way I always did whenever I went to Jerry's Music—just on the off chance that I would come across an original copy of *Yesterday and Today*. When she caught me checking her out over the tops of my records, she immediately smiled and asked me what I was looking for. I admit, I was a little smug when I said the name of the record, not the band. But she knew what it was right away, knew all about the Beatles' infamous record that had been pulled almost immediately because of its controversial cover. What's more, she had actually seen the original cover itself; a cousin of hers had the reissued version, but had managed to pull off the new cover without damaging the one underneath. We talked a lot about music that day and I couldn't believe my luck: that a girl with the face of an angel knew so much about people like Bob Dylan, and Simon & Garfunkel, and even Keith Moon. Some of the people we spent that magical first day talking about, we are going to see live over the next few days.

In the distance, I can just make out the shadows of the flimsy fences. They don't look like they are too much higher, or more complete, than when we saw them this afternoon. I hope Evan is right about not needing those tickets. I can't imagine having to turn back around after making it all this way.

I can't imagine what Amanda will do to me. I look down at her serene face again and feel a tiny shrapnel of fear go through me. I hope I won't ever have to know.

"That one there is the soupspoon," I hear Evan say, and I crane my neck to see what's going on. He's silhouetted against the moonlight, just a dark hand pointing up into the air, tracing some constellation of his imagination.

"Really?" Suzie asks from beside him, a note of disbelief in her voice.

"And that's the mashed potatoes, see the chives sticking out."

Suzie giggles, and I see her hand go up into the air too. "And I suppose that one there is the wineglass."

"Champagne flute, actually. But you seem to be getting it, baby."

I hear rather than see Suzie playfully punch Evan. "You are out of your mind, Evan Mather."

It's true. He really is.

But then again, that's usually what makes him so fun.

I realize this is the happiest I've been in a long time. The world seems infinite and my worries so small. My parents, my problems with Amanda, the looming question of what I'm going to do with my life once this summer is over—minuscule. There is only one thing that seems as substantial and weighty as the sky before me: the glorious music that will consume the next three days of my life. Hearing Jimi Hendrix pluck those strings, or Janis Joplin wail those notes, or Roger Daltrey weave a story, that's going to be what my heavens consist of.

For now, I choose not to think beyond that. I choose here and now. I'm going to choose the here and now every single moment of this weekend. Maybe that will be enough to make it last forever.

chapter 9
Cora

Dinner is a subdued affair.

I don't leave the medical tent until eight p.m. and Mom, as usual, waits for me, the meatloaf getting a little crispier than normal in the oven. Dad, naturally, grumbles about my tardiness.

I don't bother telling him that I'm pretty sure the next three nights will be even worse.

And that I'm looking forward to it. Today was the largest number of people I have ever seen. Maybe it's twisted of me to say, but I get excited thinking about the possible medical cases that could walk through the tent flap.

For most of my life, I've been certain that I want to be a nurse. The human body fascinates me, all the tiers of it, like when you scrape your knee badly and sometimes you can see layers of skin and tissue, blood and muscle. Once in the hospital I saw actual white gleaming bone.

Ned wants to be a doctor. That's how we met, actually. He used to volunteer at the hospital, just like me.

For some reason, he got to do more and see more. Probably because he's a guy and, in my candy striper uniform, I look more like some sort of sickbed cheerleader than someone serious about medicine.

Once, when he got to sit in on a heart surgery and I was relegated to getting rid of patients' wilted flowers, a seed got planted in my head.

He told me all about the surgery later. It was our idea of a hot date, him explaining the blood and valves and ligaments he saw. And I started daydreaming. Not about becoming a nurse, but about being a doctor.

I told Ned about it, once. It was after he told me about yet another surgery that he got to witness (a ruptured appendix). I said it casually, belying the way my heart was pounding near my throat. It's not that women doctors are completely unheard of. We don't have any at Community General, but I do know of one in Ellenville, about twenty miles away. But still. I wasn't sure anyone close to me would understand.

It's not that Ned said he *didn't* understand. It's not like he tried to talk me out of it, or told me it was a silly dream. He took a slight pause, just long enough for one blink behind his glasses, and then changed the subject to taking me out to the movies.

I never brought it up again. To anyone.

As I think about it now, I slice a carrot neatly in half with my butter knife, a beautiful, precise cut. I imagine I'm holding a scalpel.

"What happened to your hand?" I look up to see my dad pointing a fork at Wes's bandaged palm.

"Splinter," Wes grumbles.

My dad frowns. "Must have been an awful big splinter." Maybe inadvertently, he glances at his own arm then, the one that got shot in Korea and sent him home early, much to his dismay.

I catch the angry glint in Wes's eye and butt in. "It was. I wrapped it up."

"Hmmmph," Dad says before turning back to his loaf. I can't help but notice how both he and Wes stab their meat at the exact same moment with the exact same amount of unnecessary force.

Seems like the china is going to get the brunt end of their relationship today. Mom catches my eye and we shake our heads at each other. She gives a little sigh and I wonder if she's going to try to talk to my dad tonight. Once when I was little and the bathroom on my landing was backed up, I went upstairs to use theirs in the middle of the night and I heard them whispering to each other. I couldn't make out what they were saying, only catching all our names—Mark's, Wes's, and mine—woven throughout the conversation. I was up there for at least twenty minutes and they never stopped talking.

Even still, sometimes, it's hard for me to imagine how my parents ever got together. How my dad got home from World War II and, against his parents' wishes, married a half-Indian girl who lived on a reservation. I wonder if something in that made him go superconservative all of a sudden, like he had reached his rebellion limit by loving Mom. *Love is strange,* I think, as I move on to cutting gorgeous slices of green beans.

I hardly remember even getting into bed. I must be exhausted, because with all there is to think about—Ned, Mark, Wes, the patients, and the next three days—I fall into a deep sleep the moment my cheek touches the pillow.

Friday, August 15

chapter 10
Michael

My first thought when I wake up is that I'm being choked by a horde of yellow snakes in the wilderness of upstate New York.

I jerk up, hitting the top of Amanda's head with my chin. Her hair is tangled around my neck and shoulders.

She screams and flails her right arm, hitting me squarely in the nose. I yelp.

It's like a skit on *Benny Hill*, ending with Amanda holding her head in a dramatic fashion and yelling at me for five minutes for being a clumsy idiot.

It's during the end of her rant that I get a good look at the field around me. I swear, it's like the population has multiplied overnight, like rabbits. In fact, from my peripheral vision I'm pretty sure I can see two naked people going at it like rabbits, too. I don't bother to investigate further. (Okay, fine, so I sneak a peek at a boob freely swinging not ten feet away from me. I am an eighteen-year-old male, not a saint.)

I hear laughter and bits of conversation coming at me from everywhere.

From somewhere to my right: "I've dropped the acid, man."

"Solid."

"No, man. I literally dropped it on the ground. And I think you just stepped on it."

"Oh, shit."

From somewhere to my left: "Would you like to try some homemade granola? It's one hundred percent vegan. Remember, animals are our friends, not food."

There are kids my age as far as the eye can see. Where have they all come from suddenly in the middle of the night?

A few feet away from me, Evan and Rob emerge from the woods that surround our field. Evan has a particularly huge grin on his face. I notice that he keeps his fist closed as he walks back toward me and only opens it when he's right in front of us.

Inside are six small, shiny brown squares.

"Morning Glory," Evan identifies the batch of acid. "It's like a bitchin' pharmacy in there!" He points with his thumb to the forest behind us before popping one of the tabs onto his tongue. He lets it hang out while the tab dissolves.

Rob and the girls each take one too, the girls more demure about their tongues. I actually have never done acid before and I hesitate for a moment, looking at the last remaining tab.

"Do it for our country," Evan yells, before adding, "you yellow-bellied coward!"

I look around to see Amanda eyeing me warily, about to call me something much worse. I take the thin film and place it on my tongue.

It feels as flat and tasteless as paper. I don't know why but I expected something more, like a tingle or a metallic taste or something. I guess it's the word "acid"; it conjures thoughts of lab experiments in Chemistry.

Evan takes out his banana bunch. There just happen to be exactly six. We each take one. I'm starting to relax now, starting to feel like my usual laid-back self.

This is going to be superb. I'm going to see Joan Baez and Jimi and Grace Slick perform. We'll hang out in these beautiful fields. I'll see stars again every night.

Thinking about the stars reminds me of how I felt last night. For three days I will totally forget about the fact that I have no idea what I'm doing with my life. This is a time-out. The clock has literally stopped and there's nothing to think about but today, tomorrow, and Sunday. I can stretch out every moment to a lifetime. I can take a mental Polaroid of every single second and then expand it out into infinity. This weekend will never end and it's all because of me and my powers.

For one of those infinite split seconds, I wonder if that's the acid talking.

But then the next second comes—when I summon it to come, of course—and I realize, nah. This is all me.

I am a time god!

chapter 11
Cora

Last night, I dreamt about Ned. We were in his car, at a drive-in movie, and only half paying attention to the flickering images up on the screen. The other times, we were making out. Or just laughing and talking like normal. Like we did so many nights in the year and a half we were together.

This morning, when I wake up, it takes me a second to remember the reality of us. For just a moment, our kisses amid the scent of popcorn and leather seem like a recent memory instead of a dream. Then I hear his voice calling out to my dad downstairs and I remember. I feel betrayed by my subconscious.

I dress quickly, slipping on a simple white dress, with the intention of getting my mind occupied as soon as possible at the medical tent. But Ned has other plans. As soon as I get downstairs, he informs me that he's done helping out at our farm for the day, so of course he's going to come check out the festival too. And, of course, he's going to casually just walk over there with me.

I'm annoyed, even though it's hardly his fault that I dreamt about him. I walk briskly past our house, trying my damnedest to make the trip go as quickly as possible. We have to cross the Quickway to get over to the festival, and my jaw nearly drops at what I see. Our two-lane country street has become a virtual parking lot overnight. There are empty cars, bumper to bumper. And as we cross and get to the field on the other side, I can start to see where most of the cars' passengers must be.

"Man, this is a lot of people. Where did they all come from?" Ned says, blinking.

I was just thinking the same thing, of course, but I turn my head and glare at Ned's angular profile. I don't want him echoing my thoughts. I don't want him around at all.

"Do you even have a ticket?" I ask him, pointedly now. "The show starts tonight, so they probably won't let you in without a ticket."

"I heard they wouldn't be checking tickets," he responds breezily.

I shrug. I've heard whisperings of the same thing, but at this moment, I hope it won't be true.

"Besides," he says. "I can always come help out at the medical tents. I'm sure Anna wouldn't say no."

This is also unfortunately true. We probably need the help and Anna really likes Ned. Then again, who doesn't around here?

Why can't he disappear? Why can't breakups mean that the other person just leaves the plane of your existence entirely? I don't mean that they have to *die*. But can't they just die from your world, be obliterated from the cast of characters that populate your story, never to appear onstage with you again? And for heaven's sake, can't there be a rule banning them forevermore from your *dreams*?

"So who are you most looking forward to seeing?" Ned asks.

Nope. Instead, I'm doomed to engage in small talk with the boy who has broken my heart. And here in Bethel, I will be forced to have some version of this conversation for the rest of my existence. Today it's what act I want to see. Someday it'll be which street I'd buy my house on. That's what it means, living in a small town.

"I probably won't be seeing anybody. Pretty sure the medical tent will keep me busy," I finally respond.

"All right. Who are you looking forward to hearing?"

I shrug. "Joni Mitchell."

"Is she playing?" Ned asks.

"I thought so . . . ," I say.

"I'm pretty excited about the Who. Do you think they'll play 'My Generation'?"

"Probably. It's one of their biggest songs."

"That would be amazing." Ned smiles.

"Yeah." This field to get to the main concert area is never ending. It just goes on and on and on, swarmed with all the bright clothes and shiny, excited faces of, to quote Ned's favorite band du jour, my generation.

You know who else goes on and on and on? Ned. The boy will not stop jabbering about the concert and the music and the love and the peace and crap. I want to tell him to shut up.

I also want to make out with him.

It's all very confusing.

Finally, at long, long last, we get to the gates. I have my pass identifying me as medical personnel pinned to my dress and there actually is a glazed-over, long-bearded twenty-something standing by the gate in a red Woodstock T-shirt, theoretically on hand to check it.

"Looks like they're checking tickets," I say in a high-pitched voice.

I point to my pass as I walk by. The guy at the gate stares somewhere above and to the right of me the whole time.

I don't wait for Ned to notice, just bolt toward my medical tent, leaving him to ponder the Who's set list on his own. I think he yells out, "Hey, could you ask Anna . . ." But I ignore him. As far as I'm concerned, I don't hear a thing, so focused am I on making a beeline for the tent, where, surely, I am sorely needed.

chapter 12
Michael

Amanda is a unicorn. No, she's a dragon. No, a rainbow. No, just lightning and stars and fire.

She is everything beautiful and terrible in this world.

I am consuming her. My mouth fits around her plump lips. We are like fish, needing the motion of our mouths to breathe. If we stop, we die. So I keep going.

It's like I have infinite vision. My eyes are wide open and I can see every pore in Amanda's nose, the fine blond hairs above her lip, and the thicker ones in her eyebrows and eyelashes.

But I can also see everything going on around me. Every single person, what they are wearing, who they're with. Every fleck in the turquoise ring of the guy to the right of me. The long dark hair and red-striped dress of a girl who swishes past. Every strand of neon green grass. And I do mean every strand. I can see the water flowing through them. The molecules of chlorophyll. Hey, look, there's Chemistry again. Or is that Biology?

Biology. I can see it. I can see life itself and a strand of Amanda's saliva as she breathes it in and out against my lips. With every intake of oxygen, the strand is almost broken, only to be resurrected.

Resurrection. Like Easter. It's like Easter drool. That's what it is.

Which makes me think of Easter eggs.

Which makes me immediately pick out every pastel color I see: so many flowers on dresses to choose from. Some are peachy and some are minty.

It's been way too long since I've had Doublemint gum.

Maybe I can use some now.

Maybe Amanda can use some now. It's actually hard to tell which of us, if either, is experiencing bad-breath issues.

Though if we are sharing the same breath, does it matter?

How many breaths do we each have left anyway?

From one of my many eyes, I see a boy who can't be much older than twelve. He's with two people who look ancient, at least in their midthirties. The boy says the word "Dad."

Dad. Dad. Dad. Dadadadadadadadadadadadadad.

What a strange word. And kinda funny. But also sorta sad. But also sounding like a drum.

God, I remember being twelve. And saying "Dad." That was ages ago. So long ago and far away. It's like I was another person, and that other person is still twelve and living in 1963. And this person is in 1969. What will happen if somehow black holes collide and the old me and new me meet? Will that cause black holes to collide?

Wait, no. I said black holes collided to make the first thing happen. So that can't happen again as a cause if it's the effect.

Oh! Remember when I was the master of time? Wait, maybe I still am. I can do that again.

Can't I?

Oh my God. I've lost it. I've lost my superpower.

I've lost my youth.

"Ack! Michael!" I hear Amanda scream from above me. "What are you doing?"

The chlorophyll has the answers. I know it. It has all the molecules. It's what we are all standing on, united.

It has to be in there. My youth.

If I can just dig deep enough into this soil, I will find it. I will triumph over this temporary setback.

Someone is screaming. He sounds crazed.

Oh, wait. I think that's me. The me from two seconds ago. The me of three seconds later tells me to stop because screaming is loud and unnecessary.

But those three seconds are taking forever.

I will never stop screaming. I will never find my youth.

I will never get to the bottom of this soil.

From far above the hole I dig, I hear Evan's voice. "Oh, man, I think we have to take him to the nurse."

Rob's words echo against the millions of grass strands that are closing in around me. "He's killing my trip, man."

chapter 13
Cora

"So a little birdie told me she saw you walking with Ned earlier," Anna says to me as she dispenses two aspirin to a girl complaining of cramps.

"A little birdie? Who?"

"Maria," Anna says, indicating one of the other nurses bustling away at the back of the tent.

"Seriously? There are, like, a hundred thousand people here!" How on earth could Maria pick me out? Stupid small towns.

"So . . . is it true? Are you back together?" There's a twinkle in Anna's eye. A part of me has always felt like it wasn't just my heart that got broken when Ned and I split. I feel like I've let down my parents, Anna, and anyone else who's ever had a soft spot for Ned. So basically everyone. Except for maybe Wes.

I sigh. "No. He's just being his usual helpful self. *Helping*

my parents at the farm. *Helping* me walk across the field."
Helping me never, ever get over him.

"Well, it starts out with helping. There's a reason he's
hanging around you still, you know," Anna says confidently.

I don't want to believe it, but I'd be lying if I said that a
traitorous part of my stomach doesn't do a little flip when
Anna says that.

"TIIIIIIIIIIIIIIIIIIIIIIIIIIIIIIIIIME." Someone is bellowing.
"WHAT HAPPENED TO TIME?!"

A moment later, three guys have practically fallen into our
tent, the two on the ends hoisting up the one in the middle—I
soon realize he's the one yelling.

"It's fallen through my hands like a sieve. A SIEVE," he
practically screams in Anna's ear.

"Whoa. Okay, first of all: INDOOR VOICE, YOUNG
MAN." Anna is just as loud as the guy, and his eyes get saucer-
wide at the sound of it. I suddenly recognize him as Peach
Fuzz from the day before. In fact, I think I saw him making
out with his blond girlfriend on my way over here.

"I'm sorry," Peach Fuzz whispers.

"What's your name?" Anna asks.

"Michael," he whispers.

"And what did you take?"

Michael just shakes his head and presses his lips against
each other hard. His eyes remain huge and dilated. I don't
think he has blinked once.

Anna turns to Michael's two companions. "It's all right. He
won't get in trouble. I just need to know so we can help him."

"Acid," the taller kid says.

"What color?" Anna asks.

Both of them think about this for a moment. "I think it was brown," Rob finally says, and I realize I remember his name.

Anna notes it on her chart.

"When will it be safe to get old?" Michael whispers.

"Do we have to stay with him?" the taller kid asks, an unmistakable panic in his eyes. "The show's about to start any minute now. . . ."

He trails off as a child of maybe about eight wanders into the tent, his left knee bleeding profusely. A moment later, a short, dark-haired woman comes meandering in after him. "Think we need a Band-Aid," she says in a Southern drawl.

Unfazed as ever, Anna quickly ushers Michael toward a chair and motions for me to take some of his vitals. She then takes the mother and child to a separate corner. "Tell me what happened," I hear her ask in her matter-of-fact voice.

I make sure Michael is in place before I take my penlight and stare into his glassy eyes. If it's possible, they just get bigger. I'm surprised his tear ducts haven't kicked in by now.

I look back at his two companions and see that their panic hasn't abated in the slightest. The taller one is staring at the boy with the bloody knee and looks on the verge of a freakout himself.

"Hey, what are your names?" I ask them. "Actually, you're Rob, right?" I smile at him. I'm not likely to forget that physique anytime soon.

"Yeah . . . ," he says, eyeing me suspiciously before breaking into a grin. "Groovy. A psychic nurse."

Clearly, meeting me was not as memorable for him.

"And you are?" I turn to the very tall guy standing next to him, the one who keeps staring at the child's bloody knee.

Rob hits his companion in the elbow to get his attention.

"Evan," he finally says, tearing his eyes away from the blood.

"I'm Cora. Honestly, I think this one'll be a while, fellas," I say as I feel for Michael's pulse. "How about I keep Michael in here and you come get him at, say, around . . ." I look at my watch. It's eleven a.m. "Let's say one?"

"Oh my God," Michael says and I see him staring agape at my watch, before turning his gaze back onto me. "You have caught time. In there," he whispers as he points at my watch. "*You* are the master. How did you do it?"

"Better make that two," I say. "Can you do that? Come back at two for him?"

"Yeah," Rob says. Evan mumbles something unintelligible and then they both scramble out of there. I can almost see cartoon zoom marks in their wake. I sincerely hope they come back for Michael. It's a big farm and it won't be hard for him to lose his friends.

"Can you give time back to me?" he asks when I turn to him again.

"Sure. First, just open your mouth." I use a tongue depressor and my penlight again. Then the otoscope to check his ears.

"Okay, Michael. So here's what we're going to do. First, I'm going to give you some tea."

"Tea?" he asks.

"Yes. And then, we're going to go for a little walk just around the tent." Believe it or not, these are our actual instructions for dealing with freak-outs. Which is why Anna handed him off to me so easily. Nothing a candy striper can't handle, especially a veteran one.

I find a plastic cup and pour water out of the kettle that's being kept warm on a small gas burner. Then I take a Lipton packet out of a bin and plop it in, dunking it a few times.

"Here you go," I say. "Drink up."

Michael goes to take a sip, but then looks at me suspiciously for a moment, squinting his light green eyes. "And then . . . you'll show me?"

"I'll show you . . . ?" I wait for him to finish his thought.

"How you lassoed time?"

"Oh, yes. Definitely. Time lassoer. That's me." I have discovered in my one day working here that it's best to just go along with whatever is happening in our patients' heads. As much as soberly possible, anyway.

"Finish that and we'll have a chat all about it."

Michael looks satisfied as he takes a sip of his tea. I think I finally see him blink.

chapter 14
Michael

Two enormous brown eyes are staring into mine. Thick lashes frame them. They look like feathers. Wait, no. They *are* feathers. They are the brown circular orbs found in peacock feathers. And now they are multiplying. There were two, now four. Only this bird is red and white, with thin stripes like rivulets of deep red blood going through every feather.

Her plumage is fanning out, so many eyes and rivers. It's impossible for it to be contained.

"Tell me about your family, Michael."

Oh my God. She knows my name. This beautiful, rare bird is talking to me.

I have to do it. Very softly, I reach out and touch one of the feathers. It's like silk.

I snap my hand away like it's been burned. Idiot. I'm too impure to touch the bird. Don't I know that?

"I'm sorry," I mumble, hoping she is forgiving.

"It's all right," the bird responds calmly. "Everything will be fine. Just tell me. Start with your parents. What are their names?"

"Charles and Annemarie Michaelson."

"And do you have any siblings?"

"Just me. Michael Michaelson. Michael M. Michaelson. The M stands for Mitchell."

The bird lets out a small coo. A laugh? "You're joking."

"Never!" I yell, terrified. What happens to those who joke with a creature such as this? The words "fiery death" keep blinking on and off in my brain. "Please, I'm sorry. I wasn't." I think I can feel hot tears crawling inside my face and up my tear ducts.

"No, no," she says. "It's okay. Please don't worry."

One of her feather eyes bends down and touches my arm. I inhale sharply. It feels like a balm, reaching into my skin and drawing itself to the water in my tear ducts like a dowsing rod. Everything suddenly becomes cool and calm.

"I like it. Michael Michaelson. How did you get here, Michael?" she asks.

So I tell the bird everything. About my mother's purple Chrysler, picking up Amanda and the girls and Evan. I tell her about yesterday's burger. I hope she's proud that I didn't eat bird. Never again. Not now that I've been touched by the feathers of a goddess.

Time has stopped again. This gorgeous creature has been with me for only a millisecond. No, nine days. No, thirty-two minutes.

chapter 15
Cora

It's been six hours since Michael Michaelson was dropped off at my tent. His friends have not come back for him. He sits in a corner now while I tend to other patients. I've been keeping my eye on him, though, and it seems to me like his gaze has become just a bit more focused in the past half hour.

The sun is still blazing high in the sky when we all hear it: the very first strains of music. I look at my watch. It's a few minutes before five p.m. Quite a few anxious patients informed me that the concert was supposed to start hours ago. I can hear some of them start fidgeting now. When I look up, my eye catches Michael's. His face breaks into a grin.

I hand the cup of tea to my latest freak-out patient and walk over to him.

"How are you doing?" I ask.

He shakes his shaggy blond hair. "Okay. A little . . . groggy.

You still look a little . . . odd." He blushes then, the pink of his skin rooting to his peach fuzz and reminding me even more of the summer fruit.

"I get that a lot," I joke. I lower my voice conspiratorially. "It must be because I'm part Seneca."

"Really?" Michael's eyes get just a little brighter. "What part?"

"My grandmother," I say, surprised he's interested.

"Ah. Far out," he responds. "Do you look like her?"

Sometimes, I feel self-conscious about how obviously different I look. When I was younger, I'd compare my summer tan to my brothers' and, every now and then, wish mine wasn't quite so much darker. But I don't feel that way when I tell Michael yes, not with the way he beams at me.

We can hear some lyrics now, something about marching to the fields of Korea.

"Do you know who this is?" I ask Michael.

"I'm not sure. I thought Sweetwater was supposed to perform first, but this doesn't sound like them," he responds.

"It's Richie Havens," a blond girl drinking one of my teas offers from a corner of the tent. "I need to get out of here so I can see him."

I walk over to her with my penlight. "Okay, let me see your eyes," I say. A little glassy but focusing okay. "You feel like you can walk?"

"Definitely," she says.

"Okay, take it easy."

"Peace, sister." She gives me a hug, before taking out a pair of blue-tinted sunglasses from her shirt pocket and reaching the front flap of the tent in six long strides.

"Hey," a voice says softly from behind me. I turn around.

Michael is smiling sheepishly. "Think I'm okay to go too?"

I shine the light in his eyes, and they turn them an even lighter green, like the peridot in a ring my mother has.

"I think you're okay," I say.

"Great. Thanks. For everything. Sorry I was so messed up."

"I've seen worse," I offer.

He stares at me then for a moment too long and I wonder if he's maybe not okay to leave.

"Okay," he finally says. "Bye."

"Bye," I say, and turn around to busy myself. I can always cut more gauze strips.

I go to the bin where they're kept and grab the scissors from one of the makeshift shelves.

"Um . . . your name?" comes from somewhere right beside my ear.

I jump, nearly poking myself in the cheek with the scissors. I turn around to see Michael staring at me apologetically again.

"Sorry," he says right away. "Oh, man, I feel like 'sorry' has been half of all the words I've said to you."

I laugh. There have been a lot of other words, but he probably doesn't remember them. Not sure he wants to, either.

"It's okay."

"Kara?" he says to me. "Is that right?"

"Cora, actually."

"Sorry! Aaaah!" he slaps himself in the forehead.

"It's okay. I'm actually impressed you almost remembered. You get a B+ in freaking out."

He grins at me. I notice his two upper teeth overlap slightly. "So, Cora . . . would it be too forward of me to ask when your shift is done here?"

"Um . . . seven . . ." I hesitate. I was not expecting that. Nor am I expecting what comes out of my mouth next. "But you have to go find your girlfriend again, right?"

He blushes once more and his smile droops. "Amanda," he stammers. "Yes. Her."

"Amanda," I repeat, picturing the back of her head as I saw it that morning, in Michael's tight grasp. Then, for no reason at all, I grin like an idiot.

"Okay," he says. "Well, thank you. Again. And, for good measure, sorry." He gives me a smile before turning around and walking out of my tent.

chapter 16
Michael

Cora still has a couple of feathers sprouting from her arm when I leave her, but I choose not to bring this up with her. She's right. I need to find Amanda. And Evan, Catherine, Suzie, and Rob. I guess.

I slowly move toward the music. At certain moments, I can see trails of color undulating in time to Richie Havens's voice. He's singing a slowed-down version of "Strawberry Fields Forever" now, and some of the thousands of people around me leave pink and orange hues in their wake, including a shirtless, redheaded guy dressed in tight white pants who is gently swaying with a sheep.

"I still think the Beatles are coming, man," I hear a guy in a long purple tunic say to his friend, who just shrugs noncommittally. My sources would say: wishful thinking. Rumor has it they're on the verge of a breakup.

There are all sorts of people around me: short, tall, dark, pale, redheaded, blond, brunette, bald. A lot of people around my age, but also children and some old folks. Even when I visited Times Square with my family three years ago, I never saw this many people all in one place.

There is one problem. None of them are my friends. And as I slowly trudge my way closer to the music, I cannot fathom how I will ever find them. This is an ocean of heads and bodies. How can you find five specific drops of water in an ocean? Just when I start mulling that impossibility, I catch a glimpse of red and white from the corner of my eye, and immediately whip around. Only when I see that it's some stranger in a striped dress do I remember that Cora is not the one I'm supposed to be looking for. "Get it together, Michaelson," I mutter.

Eventually, I make it as close as I think I can get to the stage for now. It sits at the bottom of a hill, level with me, but I see that a lot of the audience is camped out on various parts of the slope, staring down into the stage like a crystal ball. Havens is a hazy orange blob who stands at the center in front of a microphone and, I think, is brandishing a guitar.

It's taken me all this time to realize that I am actually inside the festival, despite the lack of tickets. I silently thank Evan—wherever he is—for however he made that happen.

And then I just close my eyes for a moment and listen. As Havens sings about freedom, I think about my own. Freedom from my parents. From Amanda. From school, and the war, and even the limits I put on myself. Why can't I be anything, go anywhere? What is there to stop me?

Thinking about going anywhere only brings one image to my mind. I open my eyes and slowly turn my head to find it: the yellow medical tent. It's far away now, even farther than the stage. But somehow I realize the thing that's been bobbing up and down just below the surface of my thoughts is the long dark hair of a part-Seneca girl.

I look around and, after a few moments, spot a girl with a slim Timex on her wrist. "Excuse me, could you give me the time?" I ask her.

"Six thirty," she says gleefully, her eyes shining with the same sort of warmth toward mankind I can see in most of the faces surrounding me.

"Thanks," I say, reflecting her feelings back at her.

I amble back to my yellow landmark, trying to take as close to half an hour as possible, and not even looking for the flash of blond hair I'm supposed to find. Richie is singing about freedom and this is mine, a yellow that is full of possibility instead of weight.

chapter 17
Cora

I bandage up my last bloody foot (these people really need to stop walking around barefoot) and tell Ruth, who relieved Anna about twenty minutes ago, that I'm off for the day. She gives me a brief nod of acknowledgment before turning back to her latest patient, a guy who must be in his sixties at least. I admire his tenacity even as I think him a great big idiot for being in the middle of this overcrowded field at his age.

There's music when I walk out of the tent, but no singing. Instead, I hear a gentle voice reverberating throughout the fields. Some guru is giving a speech about celestial sounds and the universe and vibrations. "The future of the whole world is in your hands," his voice echoes across the field.

"Hey," a voice says near my ear. I turn around and see, to my surprise, Peach Fuzz.

"Michael," I say. "What are you doing here? Are you feeling

okay?" I squint into his eyes. They look clear and bright.

He laughs. "Yes. I came to enlist your services. Though not your nursing services."

I stare at him blankly and he clears his throat nervously. "I just mean," he continues, "I thought I'd invite you to the concert."

"Invite me?" I can't help laughing. "How kind of you." The roots of his stubble turn pink. I really didn't mean to embarrass him. "What about your friends?" I ask, remembering the blonde again.

"I can't find them," he confesses.

"Ah," I say. Being invited to a concert I'm already at by a boy who is only doing it because he's missing his girlfriend. This might be a new low.

"Wait," Michael says, touching my wrist. "That's not what I meant. I mean, me not finding my friends is not why I want to go to the concert with you."

"It isn't?"

"No," he says solemnly. "I figured it would be good to have a nurse around in case I have a flashback." He waits for a beat before breaking into a grin. "I'm just being an ass," he admits.

"I'll say." But I can't help smiling at him. "Anyway, I'm not a nurse yet. Just a candy striper." I indicate my ridiculous uniform.

"Well, you're good at it," he replies easily. "And seriously, I would just like to listen to some music with you. Is that all right?"

I admit there is something sheepdog-adorable about him as he stands there staring down at me with smiling green eyes, both hands jammed into the pockets of his bell-bottoms.

But then I think of all the reasons to say no. It's been a long day already. Dinner is waiting for me at home. Besides, how will I tell my parents if I decide to stay? There's a small pay-phone bank nearby but I can see how far the lines for that stretch back. It'll take three hours just waiting in that line to call them. And Dad will definitely be sending out a search party by that point.

"N . . ." I say the letter, intending it to start the word no. But then it makes a different, heart-sinking word. "Ned." He's walking toward me and waving. Michael turns around to look at him.

"Hey there," Ned says. "Getting ready to pack it in for the night?"

He smiles at me and my lungs hurt. Okay, so it's probably a different organ that's in the vicinity of my lungs, but it somehow makes me feel less pathetic to think I spontaneously have a respiratory problem.

But then Ned's trademark know-it-all smile steals across his face. "See? They're not checking tickets at all. Everybody can get in. Like I said."

My respiratory problem is interrupted by a surge of anger that jolts the next words out of my mouth. "Hey, Ned. Are you heading back home soon?"

"Right now, I think. I can walk you home if you'd like."

From the corner of my eye, I can see Michael staring rather intensely at Ned and, I have to admit, a part of me is feeling very pleased about it.

"No need," I say slowly. "Actually, I was wondering if you could do me a favor. Could you just stop by my parents' house and let them know that I'm going to be at the concert for a while? I don't want them to worry."

Ned's eyebrows furrow in confusion. "You are?" he asks.

"Yup."

"But I thought you said—"

"See you later!" I cut him off as I grab Michael's arm and saunter away toward the stage. I have to settle for imagining Ned's stunned face since I won't give him the satisfaction of turning around to look at it.

Pompous ass. I will get over him somehow and my alveoli will go back to properly distributing oxygen and carbon dioxide. And in the meantime, I'm going to stop thinking of all the reasons to say no to the cute boy who has not really asked me out at all.

This is a weekend for yeses. And thousands of people agree with me as I hear them chanting, in unison, "Hari Om, Hari Om" over and over again. I don't know the language but I somehow know exactly what they are saying.

Yes. Yes. Yes.

chapter 18
Michael

Not that it's any of my business, but I don't particularly like the way that guy with the glasses looks at Cora, like she's a casual possession. A small but useful possession. Like an alarm clock or something.

I don't particularly like the way she looked back at him either.

What is wrong with me? I met this girl about ten hours ago, six of which I can hardly remember. It must be the side effects of the acid.

Regardless, Cora still holds my arm as we wade through the crowd, her black hair floating behind her like a panel of silk. And I'm keenly aware of both of those things, especially the touch of her hand on my forearm. It's rougher than most girls' hands I've held and, for some reason, I'm finding this pretty damn sexy.

"So who are you excited to see?" I ask her, finding the most readily available topic.

"Umm . . ." She hesitates. This whole thing is in her backyard and she doesn't automatically know the answer to that? "Joni Mitchell?" she says haltingly.

"Really? Is she playing?"

"I thought so . . ." Cora drifts off, and I think I hear her mutter, "Déjà vu."

I don't remember seeing Joni on the roster, and I think I have it pretty well memorized, but I decide to let it go. Besides, we're getting closer to the stage now and the sound of a man and woman singing together envelopes us.

I see Cora squint toward the stage, trying to figure out the faraway figures.

"Sweetwater." I offer the name of the band. "Not huge yet but I think they might be."

Cora looks at me. For a moment, I think she might be offended that I showed her up like that. Offered her information she didn't already know. Amanda would have been.

But instead she just grins. "Thanks," she says. "I really should know more about this stuff."

I smile back. Without thinking, I go to move her hand off my arm and shift it so that our fingers interlace instead.

She looks at our clasped hands quizzically but doesn't pull away.

Sweetwater is playing a groovy flute solo and my eyes are drawn back to them. They are an odd band: flute, keyboards, cello. And their lead singer, a slight girl—even slighter from where I stand—is swaying freely to the high-pitched notes.

I notice we are swaying slightly too and so are most of the people around us, like reeds blowing in the same wind.

The ethereal piping is suddenly interrupted by a loud, totally unwelcome rumbling.

Cora immediately looks up to the cloudy sky. "Thunder?" she asks.

I, instead, stare down at myself. "My stomach," I finally admit, a little embarrassed.

Cora follows my gaze and laughs. "When was the last time you ate?"

"Umm . . ." I rack my brain. "Does tea count?"

"No." Cora emphatically shakes her head. "And I'm surprised you even remember that."

"If it makes you feel better, I'm pretty sure I thought it was unicorn tears," I offer.

"Ah. Makes a lot more sense. And how did that taste?"

I scratch my stubble with my free hand. "Kind of like a rainbow. Trapped in an orange rind. If that makes any sense."

Cora cocks her head. "Nope," she says.

"It would if you'd been on what I was on."

"Thank God for both of us I wasn't. Or who would have served you unicorn tears that tasted like rainbows and oranges?"

"Orange rind," I correct, and at the words, my stomach gives another huge rumble. Because apparently there's nothing more appetizing than some tasty orange rind.

"Come on," Cora says, tugging me away from the stage. "To the food tents."

chapter 19
Cora

Come to think of it, I haven't eaten in a while either. I brought half a ham sandwich from home with me. When did I have that? Around two? Too long ago to count.

The food tents are purple and are set up at the top of the hill that leads to the stage. The line to them snakes around a few times and it takes us a while to find the end of it.

"You've come to the right place," says a somewhat tubby guy with an Australian accent when he sees us looking around for where to get in line. He smiles and points right behind himself with fingers that have silver rings on each and every one.

"Thanks," Michael says. And then, after a moment, "Where are you from?"

"Sydney, Australia," the guy says. Then a short woman with hair almost to her feet calls out, "Nate . . ." and he turns his attention to her.

"And I thought traveling from Massachusetts was far," Michael says.

I laugh. "No one has a longer commute than me."

"Oh, yeah. What is it? Three feet?"

"Excuse me," I say, pretending to be affronted. "It's half a mile. *At least.*"

"You sure you don't want to sit down? Rest your feet?" Michael stares down at my sensible Keds.

"Um, it's not as if you actually *walked* from Massachusetts."

"I might as well have! Do you have any idea how far back my car is?"

"Three feet?" I counter sweetly.

Michael grins. "Half a mile at least. Maybe even two halves of a mile . . ." He drifts off as he realizes what he's saying. "So, like, one mile."

"Impressive math skills," I laugh.

"Hey!" A voice says from behind me and I turn around to see Wes, *sans* protest sign this time.

"Hey," I say. And then I check my watch. It's almost eight thirty p.m. "Wait," I say, a small panic starting to set in. "You didn't go home for dinner either?"

Wes looks at me as if I've lost my mind. "You want me to leave this for dinner?"

"Did you tell Mom and Dad you wouldn't be home?"

"No," he says without any hesitation.

I sigh. Great. Now they'll be worried about him, and my absence will be even more obvious.

I look over at my lanky brother and see him eyeing the

even lankier Michael. I guess I'd better go ahead and introduce them.

"Wes, this is Michael. Michael, Wes. Wes is my brother," I say, not bothering to further elaborate on my relationship to Michael.

Not that Wes doesn't pick up on that. "Her twin brother," he says, in an oddly menacing voice.

"Oh, really?" Michael says, shaking Wes's hand. "Cool. Twins." He looks back and forth between us for a second. "You don't . . ."

"Look alike?" Wes butts in. "Yeah, we know."

Michael gives an easy grin. "Well, no. You don't. But I'm guessing that's because Cora looks better in a dress."

I sputter out a laugh. Wes seems less amused. I can already see that obnoxious-protective brother glaze taking over his eyes. "Wait, how do you guys know each other again?"

"Oh, from around," I say just as Michael chirps in with "We met at the medical tents."

Wes's scrutiny turns solely to me. "Oh, great. Another doctor wannabe, Cora?"

"No." I scowl. "He's just a music . . . person. Like a friend."

"A music friend? What does that mean?"

"It means . . ." I honestly have no idea. But luckily I'm saved from the rest of the embarrassing conversation by our Australian buddy.

"No point standing around here anymore, mates." Yes, he actually says "mates." "They are all out of food."

"Wait, what?" Michael says. "Are you serious?"

"'Fraid so," says Nate. And sure enough, the line is dispersing with a lot of grumbles and talk of what to do to feed starving bellies.

"Wow," I say, pretty stunned.

"Wow," Wes echoes.

"Well," Michael says slowly. "At least now I'm beginning to see the twin thing."

chapter 20
Michael

I'm not feeling so hot. Kind of floaty and light-headed. I look wistfully at the useless food tents. It really has been forever since I've eaten. Was it a banana I had this morning? And some tea?

I see Cora looking at me with nursely concern. "We could go back to my place," she offers. "I'm sure my parents could add one for dinner."

She sounds unsure and I hear her brother snort lightly.

It's very sweet of her but, to be honest, I didn't come all this way to miss the concert and sit down with some random chick's parents. I've never even had dinner with Amanda's parents.

I plaster on a smile. "Nah. I'll be fine," I say, and then look out over in the direction of the music. "Let's go get closer to the stage?"

Cora hesitates and for a second I'm sure she's going to say no. Instead, she looks over at her brother. "See you later," she says to him, before turning to me and cocking her head toward the sound of a piano.

"Don't forget your curfew," Wes grumbles behind us.

"Thanks, *Dad*," Cora says, before rolling her eyes at me. I smile as we walk down the hill, where the stage sits like Glinda's bubble from *The Wizard of Oz*, pulsating magic.

"Sorry about Wes," Cora says. "Sometimes he just gets overprotective. Twin brother thing or something."

"No problem," I say.

"He gets weird around me and guys. Never liked Ned either . . ." She trails off.

It's cool. I really don't need to know this girl's whole story. "Is Ned the guy from before? The guy with the glasses?" But apparently my mouth doesn't feel the same way.

"Yeah," Cora says, looking straight ahead and sort of shrinking into herself. Maybe she's purposely not meeting my eye. But why should that matter to me? She is my . . . what did she call it? Oh, yeah, music buddy. For the day.

"Is that your ex?" I blurt out. Goddamn it, Michaelson. What the hell?

"Um. Yeah." She turns to me this time. "Ex," she says as if she wishes that weren't the word she had to use for him. I find myself wishing she didn't sound so down in the dumps about it.

But this whole thing is ridiculous. I shake my head to clear it of its nonsensical thoughts, determined to enjoy the rest of the show with an empty mind. And an extremely empty stomach, apparently.

By the time we get near the stage, Tim Hardin has just finished playing and the stage is being set up for the next performer. I squint until I see him waiting on the sidelines, a black-haired man wearing a long white tunic and carrying a tall stringed instrument that ends in a round, squat wooden head.

"Ravi Shankar," I announce, and am glad for it. I can use some meditative sitar music right now to float me away from the physical. In this case, my hunger pains.

I close my eyes as Ravi sits down and tunes his instrument. Just as he plucks his first few notes and I'm getting ready to lose myself to some higher state of being or whatever, something extremely hard and fast hits me in the back of my head.

"Ow!" I turn around to confront whoever has just assaulted me.

"Oh, man. I'm so sorry, man!" A guy with a long black beard is looking over at me in horror. "I didn't mean . . . I just thought you might want some sustenance."

He points down at my foot and I look to see the culprit behind what is likely to be a very large lump on my head. It's a beautiful, perfect, big (and heavy) orange.

I look back up at the guy, stunned. "For me?" I ask stupidly.

Blackbeard nods. "For sure, man."

I pick the fruit up. It even feels delicious, its pockmarked skin heavy with juice.

"Are you sure?" I have to ask again, especially as I've just noticed the very pregnant woman sitting down on the blanket right at his feet.

"Definitely," he says. "We have to feed each other out here, dude. Peace and love and music, right? Besides, it's the least I could do for conking you in the head with it."

I stare down at the woman again, who keeps one hand on her belly as she waves the other one at me in a friendly gesture. "Take it with our blessings," she says. And then I see her take out three more oranges from a canvas bag she has beside her. She hands them up to her man, who starts walking around, giving them out to other people.

I look down at the orange and for a second feel like Ravi is picking out the music straight from inside me: the immense crescendo of gratitude and peace and awe toward my fellow man seems interpreted exactly in the swell of his sitar strings.

I look up at Cora and grin.

chapter 21
Cora

I think the last time I saw someone staring at something the way Michael is staring at that orange was a Christmas morning when Wes got the green army men he'd been coveting for half the year. The irony of which is not lost on me.

Michael peels into his orange slowly, staring at it as if it might disappear at any moment.

"Don't worry, it's not a hallucination," I say as he reverently excavates the fruit from the skin.

He breaks it open into two sections and then gallantly holds his hand out with one of them cradled inside.

I laugh. "You're kidding, right? Eat the whole thing."

"But you must be starving too."

"I'm not. And besides, I thought we established that I live three feet over that way. On a *farm*. Where there is all sorts of food and food-producing things."

Michael stares at the half orange he's holding out to me again. "Please?" he says.

"Michael. I appreciate the ridiculous chivalry but come on." I push his hand back toward him. "What kind of a nurse would I be if I deprived my patient of food when he's about to pass out from hunger?"

"I thought you said you were a candy striper?" Michael grins.

"Oh, fine. Rub it in." I stare pointedly at the orange. "This candy striper is medically ordering you to eat."

Michael carefully peels off one orange section and plops it in his mouth. He can't help but close his eyes as the juice hits his taste buds. A slow, savoring smile creeps stealthily through his peach fuzz.

Until there's a rumble and his eyes immediately pop open and go to my stomach. "See? I told you . . . ," he starts.

There is another loud rumble and we both look up, knowing full well it isn't either of our stomachs this time.

A big fat raindrop plops down right on my nose, followed by one more. Until, suddenly, it's like there's a tear in the sky and a deluge has been unleashed upon O little town of Bethel.

I hear a collective squawk as people try to take shelter. Some are burrowing into sleeping bags or putting newspapers over their heads. A few enterprising individuals had the foresight to bring umbrellas and are popping them open now. There is a mass exodus toward some trees on the far side of the field.

But for most people, there is simply nowhere to go.

"Hopefully it'll pass soon," I hear the pregnant girl with

the oranges say placidly as she remains on her blanket, absentmindedly rubbing her belly.

I look down at my once white dress, which is basically now completely transparent. Hastily, I take my red-and-white apron from my arm and put it on, though not before I spy Michael getting a good long look. Within moments, the individual stripes are indiscernible; it just looks like one soggy pink mess. I guess I'm giving the people behind me a show since the apron doesn't cover my back. But then I look around at the many, many other young women wearing white shirts, a lot of them braless, and figure they'll have better things to stare at than me.

Though when I look up again at Michael, he doesn't seem to have figured this out yet, his eyes only on me. A sly grin he can't seem to hide fast enough appears through his stubble again. I clear my throat, making a mental note to keep only my front to him at all times.

I realize then that the music hasn't stopped for even a moment; the man on stage keeps picking out his intricate tune despite the world turning into a waterfall around him. I watch him in awe.

It's minutes later that I even think to look at my watch. It's still working despite the water. Ten thirty. My curfew is eleven. I really should go.

I look up at Michael, who is drenched, his own shirt sticking tightly to every definition in his lean body. He's staring raptly at the stage.

I touch his arm gently. "I think I have to go home," I say.

"Oh," he says, not able to hide the disappointment in his voice. "Of course. Yes. It's horrible out here."

"Are you going to be okay?"

"Oh, totally. I didn't really mean horrible. I mean, it's just some rain. It's actually wonderful." He gestures toward the stage. "I wouldn't miss this for anything."

"Right," I say, trying to figure out how exactly to say good-bye. I mean, once I do, I'll probably never see him again.

A man with a megaphone is walking around repeating, "The flat blue acid is poison. Don't take the flat blue acid."

A look of panic steals into Michael's eyes. "Wait, did I . . ." He trails off.

"It wasn't blue," I say. "I don't think."

"Oh. Okay." He smiles at me but his eyes remain worried.

I look at the tall, soaking-wet boy in front of me, who suddenly looks so much smaller and more helpless than he has any right to. And then I look down at my soggy apron.

How can I leave him really? As a candy striper. No, as a medical professional. Someday anyway.

I move closer to him and touch his arm. "You'll be okay," I say. "I'll stay with you and make sure."

The relief in his eyes is palpable. I wonder if he can see the relief in mine. Or the inexplicable gratitude I suddenly feel for the once red and white bands of my uniform.

chapter 22
Michael

Water does wondrous things to white clothing. I'm not sure I realized that before. There's no way Cora hasn't caught me checking her out but I can't help it. She's a medical person. She must understand the afflictions of a teenage boy to some extent.

I'm also glad she's here because, truthfully, I'm a little freaked out about the acid. Under no circumstance can I even remotely remember what color tab I took. Cora said it wasn't blue, but she hadn't looked so sure.

Then again, it has led her to stay. I reach out and lightly hold on to her wrist for reassurance. I also silently will it not to sprout more feathers.

In between sets, I catch a glimpse of Cora's brother again. He's with a small group, holding up signs. His once read END THE WAR NOW in a patriotic red and blue, with stars and stripes decorating the corners. It hasn't fared too well in the rain, though; its edges are curled over and some of the paint on the words has started to run. But only the red paint, for some reason, which means that the word "war" is now a dripping, barely legible mess.

"End the Blob Now!" I say.

"What?" Cora asks.

"Oh." I've just realized I said that out loud. "Nothing. Just your brother's sign." I point over to it. "The rain. And the word 'war' . . ." I drift off. The explanation sounds even dumber than the outburst.

But Cora laughs. "Yeah," she says. "Might as well be a blob though, huh? The way it's going over there in Vietnam. The way nobody seems to know what the hell they're doing." She takes in a sharp breath. I guess the antiwar thing runs in the family.

"It does seem like a mess," I offer.

Cora nods. "My other brother is over there," she says softly. "Mark."

"I'm sorry."

"Me too," she agrees with a sad smile but then, thankfully, seems to have nothing more to say on the subject. In my experience, nothing good ever comes out of me getting into a deep discussion about the war. I feel too ambivalent about it to contribute much and I always somehow end up offending whomever I'm talking to—no matter what side they're on.

Before I know it, the singer known simply as Melanie is being introduced and is warbling gently through the rain about beautiful people she hasn't met before today. Which leads my mind to much more pleasant subjects. Like the one beautiful person with hair like silk who is standing next to me, holding my hand, now studded with raindrops sparkling in the moonlight.

Melanie sings about never meeting her beautiful stranger again. I look over at mine and hope it won't be true.

chapter 23
Cora

I'm surprised my watch is still working, considering all the rain that must be getting into it, but I actually see the minute hand move from 11:19 to 11:20. Wow. I really need to get home.

I take my sodden hair in one hand and twist it around to wring the water out, knowing perfectly well it's futile. But turning my head gives me a good guise for looking over at Michael. He's watching the singer onstage in raptures.

What am I going to do with him? I've already tried to leave him once and couldn't. But if I don't get home soon, my father will literally send out a search party. That blond guy making the announcements will be up there at the mic, calling my name, telling me to go home. And I will actually die of embarrassment. Really. I can just picture the rain mixing with the waves of humiliation radiating off me to create a toxic gas that will kill me and everyone within a ten-foot radius of me. It'll be Woodstock's great tragedy. A morbid smirk spreads across my face.

I peek again at Michael and in my haze of insane thoughts, another one takes hold.

It's absolutely crazy. I don't know if he'll even entertain it. And even if he does, I know for a fact that the logistics of it will be a nightmare.

"Hey, I have to go home," I find myself saying to him. But before his eyes fully dilate to puppy dog, I blurt out, "Do you want to come with me? I could get you something to eat and a bed." I flush immediately at what I've seemingly just offered. "I mean, your own bed. Well, more likely a couch. Just . . . a place to sleep. Is what I meant."

Lovely.

Michael opens his mouth and then turns to look longingly at the stage. I can see the word "no" forming on his lips. And then, to my surprise, he turns back to me and says, "Yes. I'll walk back with you."

He smiles and I smile back, despite the fact that my stomach is now doing flip-flops at the prospect that a) I have just asked a strange boy back to my house where b) my father lives and c) I will have to think of a way to sneak him in and out of there and d) also feed him.

He squeezes my hand as we turn around and slowly make our way through the crowd.

"I can't wait to finally see this farm," he says. "You've been going on and on about it for ages."

"Yes," I counter. "All six hours we've known each other."

"Hey! I thought we met this morning. It's been at least twelve hours."

"I don't think those first six hours count, since I'm pretty sure you thought I was a bird or something."

Michael goes a little red. "I said something about that?" he says in a small voice.

I laugh. "Don't worry. It was all very charming. And complimentary," I can't help adding. "Anyway, I like birds. We have chickens at home."

"Delicious," Michael says.

"Don't let me catch you saying that in the henhouse. They are very sensitive."

Despite what my miraculous watch continues to tell me, we don't hurry while making our way out of the concert grounds. The singers have changed again by the time we make it to the edge, and someone I actually recognize is now onstage: Arlo Guthrie.

"I don't know, like, how many of you can dig, like, how many people there are, man." Arlo's voice is fading out. "Man, there are supposed to be a million and a half people here by tonight. Can you dig that? The New York State Thruway is closed, man." He laughs. "A lot of freaks!"

A million and a half freaks. In Bethel. Unreal. And absolutely fantastic. I *can* dig it.

chapter 24
Michael

Holy Christ. I don't know what happened in the last day, but if I thought my car was the only one pulled over on the main road, I was dead wrong. There are rows upon rows of empty cars, joyfully abandoned in the middle of the street. It looks like an alien abduction scene from *The Twilight Zone*.

"That's a first," Cora says as she points down the road.

"What? Bethel isn't normally a parking lot?"

"Definitely not. But I was actually talking about the little market that's down there." She points down the street, where I can see the lights on in a small building with a long line snaking out of it. It looks like someone is at the door, monitoring how many people enter and leave.

"Is it usually open this late?" I ask.

Cora laughs. "Nothing in Bethel is open this late. Until this weekend anyway."

We are on the other side of the street and, as we pass it, I glance into the shop's windows. Rows upon rows of empty metal shelves gleam in the moonlight.

"Wow," Cora says, eyebrows furrowing with worry. "I hope everyone will be okay. With food and everything."

"How long can people survive without food anyway?" I ask her.

"Well, technically, a few weeks. Water is a different issue, though," she responds.

"I think we might be okay on water," I say, holding my hand up and letting raindrops collect in it.

"Yeah, I guess you're right." She pauses. "Of course, then there's the matter of catching a cold. Or pneumonia."

"You medical people are just a garden of optimism, eh?" I tease.

"Just prepared for all eventualities," she says. "It's a fine quality to have in a doctor, trust me."

A couple of buildings past the market, we make a right, and walk down a large stretch of farmland dotted here and there with big houses. She holds my hand until we see a large gray house come into view. Then she takes her hand back and wipes it nervously on her dress.

"So . . . about getting into my house . . . ," she starts to say as we walk under a big leafy maple at the foot of the driveway.

But then the screen door slams open and I hear a gruff voice call out, "Cora Eloise Fletcher. That better be you out there and you better have an outstanding explanation as to why you're coming home at *midnight*."

Cora looks at me in mortification. I immediately sink back within the shadows of the tree trunk and try to nod at her encouragingly, telling her to go.

She nods slightly, takes a deep breath, and steps into the light spilling out the front door. "Hi, Dad."

"Hi, Dad? That's it? That's all you have to say to me?"

"Things ran really late at the medical tent and there were people that needed help . . . ," Cora starts.

"And there were medically trained *adults* there to help them. What business does a seventeen-year-old girl with a curfew have being there this late? With all the drunken, drugged-up louses desecrating our land? Are you out of your mind, girl?"

"Technically, it's Mr. Yasgur's land," I hear Cora grumble.

"What?" her dad says sharply.

"Nothing, Dad. I'm sorry. It won't happen again."

"You can bet your bottom dollar it won't happen again," he says as Cora slowly trudges by him. "This is unacceptable, irresponsible behavior and I won't stand for it." The door slams shut behind them, but I can hear his voice fading away as he must be following Cora down some sort of hallway. "Just because Max Yasgur thinks it's okay to invite the entire country to destroy our farms doesn't mean my kids get to suddenly do whatever they want. . . ."

Yikes. Suddenly I'm a little glad my father is the silent type.

The tree shades me from the rain at least, but I'm not sure what to do. Obviously, I have to get back to the festival soon, but if I leave now, I won't have said good-bye to Cora at all.

What if I leave and she comes back out here looking for me? On the other hand, it doesn't sound like her dad is likely to let her out of his sight soon. And on yet a third hand— foot?—how long will I have to wait before I'm certain she's not coming?

I don't have a watch so I decide to count slowly to two hundred. If she doesn't get out here by then, I'll just call it a night.

At seventy-three, I hear the click of a latch. Cora stands in front of a fence, about twenty feet to the right of me. She puts her finger to her lips and waves me over.

Walking as quietly as I can, I keep a nervous eye on the front door of her house.

She takes my hand, reopens the latch on her fence, and takes me through to a barn that's standing on the far side of her backyard. We go to the side that's facing away from the house before she speaks.

"I'm really sorry about that," she whispers.

"Please, don't apologize. Parents. I've got them too." I smile.

"Yeah, of course. Still, I'm sorry." She furrows her brow again, which I'm starting to recognize as her worried-nurse look. "Listen, I would totally let you stay in here." She points to the barn. "But the animals will cause a ruckus and then my dad . . ."

I grab her hand. "Hey, it's okay. I totally understand. And anyway, I wasn't going to spend the night here."

"You weren't?" she asks.

"No. I just said I'd walk you home. I can't miss the festival."

"Oh," she says. "Right. Of course." She almost sounds disappointed but I can't figure out why. Wasn't she just trying to get me out of here herself? Women are confusing.

"But look, how about we meet tomorrow? What do you think?" I say.

"Tomorrow?"

"Yeah, were you still planning on being there?" I just assumed she would be but maybe that wasn't so bright.

"Yeah, I'm working the medical tent again."

"Oh," I say. "Well, maybe I can just come see you there? Just to say hi?" That sounds stupid.

But she smiles. "That would be nice. And actually, I start work at eleven. Do you maybe want to meet up earlier? Like around nine?"

"That would be great," I say, a wave of relief washing over me. "At your medical tent?"

Cora nods and then pulls up one of her hands. In it is a half-filled bag of Wonder Bread and a solid bit of something wrapped up in waxed paper.

"Dinner's on me," she says.

I take the papered package and peek inside to find a hunk of cheese. "And will I ever meet the lady that produced this?" I ask, pointing to the barn.

"Maybe someday. If you're good," she says without missing a beat.

"Seriously, though. Thank you so much," I start.

"Don't. It's nothing." She hands over the bag of bread. "I have to go, though. Otherwise, I won't be let out of the house for a nine a.m. meeting with anyone over the next ten to fifteen years."

"Thank you," I say again and then, before I can change my mind, I lean down and lightly kiss her lips. It's quick, a peck at most, but I feel my pulse speed up as I back away and look at her.

She looks surprised but gives me a shy grin when she says, "See you tomorrow."

"See you," I say as I quietly go back through the fence, my hands heavier with glorious food, and my head lighter with the electric touch of her lips.

chapter 25
Cora

I don't take any more chances after Michael leaves me at the barn. I hurry back inside, and I'm in my nightgown and in bed less than ten minutes later so that in case my father checks in, there won't be anything more he can grumble about.

I sigh at the thought of my dad, still feeling a little embarrassed at everything Michael heard. I don't know what I expected, though. I couldn't have scripted that conversation any more accurately if I'd tried. Why didn't I give the lecture a thought when I invited Michael back to the house?

Maybe because it all felt so . . . nice. To have someone look at me like that, listen to me. I haven't felt like the center of someone's attention in a long time, probably since the first few months with Ned. Plain and simple, Michael is fun. Between worrying about things like the future, or disappointing my parents, or Mark, maybe I've forgotten what it is to actually have fun. Not that Mark can ever be too far from my thoughts, really. The idea of him being blown to smithereens is imprinted on my brain at this point, and no boy—no matter how cute, or scruffy, or charming—can entirely wipe that clean.

And yet, the thing that should have been most fun of all— that sweet little kiss—is the one thing that's bringing on all sorts of overwhelming memories. About Ned.

That's right: Michael kisses me and all I can do is think of my ex-boyfriend. How unfair is that?

It's probably because Ned is the last person I kissed, just two hours before he broke my heart, and the touch of someone else's lips on mine now floods my mind with memories of that entire night.

The sound of crickets and cicadas in the air, the smell of mown grass mingling with fireworks. Smoke hanging in the air from the Fourth of July celebrations, streaking the sky like fingerprints on a car window. We were right under the maple tree in my front yard, only a few steps away from the barn, when he started talking about how difficult things would be when he was away at college in the fall and I was still stuck here finishing up my senior year of high school. He didn't think that it made sense for us to put ourselves through a long-distance relationship when we both had other things we should be focusing on. He told me that we needed some time apart.

That's how he said it: "*We* need some time apart." Not just him. Because that's the way things work in Ned's world: What's right for him is right for everyone. And I know that about him, and it's irritating as all get-out. So why, then, am I lying in my bed and missing the feel of his lips on mine, when someone new and exciting, someone whose annoying habits I haven't yet gotten to know, has just had his lips there too? Why do I feel pangs of longing for the way Ned's glasses slid forward and touched the bridge of my nose when he leaned into me, a piece of glass and plastic that suddenly felt so intimate between us, like it was imbibed with our heartsong?

I roll over and let out an angry huff of air. This is childish and unproductive. Instead, I should think about what sort of food I can bring with me tomorrow to help out. Maybe I can hard-boil some eggs. We have at least two other loaves of bread that I can take, and I can bake some more to make up for it. There is plenty of cheese in the pantry that my father won't miss.

I drift off as I make a checklist of things to do and the last thing I think about is, in fact, Michael. I wonder if he will actually find me tomorrow morning at nine. And then I think about him in the rain and hope he'll be okay.

I'll make sure to save some extra food just for him.

chapter 26
Michael

I savor every bite of that cheese. It's cheddar, I think, sharp and delicious especially when placed in hunks between a rolled-up piece of Wonder Bread. I think this may have just knocked last night's burger out of contention for the top five meals of my lifetime.

The grocery store has shuttered its doors for good by the time I walk past it again. If they're smart, they won't bother opening up in the morning. Unless they magically get a new shipment of supplies in.

I'm down to my last two slices of bread by the time I can hear the music again. A woman's voice is faintly drifting over, getting louder as I walk past the half-finished gates.

Vaguely, I keep an eye out for Evan and Amanda, thinking it might be nice to find them again at some point. But if I'm honest with myself, I don't look very hard.

The field by the stage is still packed, but this time with prone bodies, some in sleeping bags and on blankets. Some not so lucky.

I'm going to have to be one of the latter if I can't find my friends.

I recognize Joan Baez's unmistakable voice once I reach the top of the big hill. It slides over me like moth wings, at once tangible and translucent.

I walk slowly down toward the stage. Joan finishes her song and starts talking about her husband and how he's been in jail for years for protesting the war. "I was happy to find out that after David had been in jail for two and a half weeks, he already had a very, very good hunger strike going with forty-two federal prisoners, none of whom are draft people," she says.

It's still too dark to see her but I feel a pang of jealousy for all the conviction in her voice, and all the conviction that must be in her husband's. I wish I felt that strongly about something.

At least I can appreciate the music. I find a tree to lean against, and let it wash over me as Joan sings, this time without any musical accompaniment. Just her pure voice ringing out, "Swing low, sweet chariot, coming for to carry me home."

She sings one more song before leaving the stage to loud applause and whistles. Then a man's deep voice comes over the sound system.

"That brings us fairly close to the dawn," he says. "Maybe the best thing for everyone to do, unless you have a tent or someplace specific to go to, is carve yourself out a piece of territory, say good night to your neighbor. And say thank you to yourself for making this the most peaceful, the most pleasant day anybody's ever had in this kind of music."

There is more applause and whistles and I can feel a wave of instant nostalgia wash over the audience as everyone reflects on their pleasant, peaceful, perfect day. I catch the eye of a short guy standing next to me and he nods at me in a gesture of camaraderie. Then he salutes me before walking a few steps over and settling himself down on the ground. More and more heads are starting to disappear from view, and it's clearly time for me to follow suit.

I sink right down into the mud. At least it's soft. I use the root of the tree as a sort of pillow, my body now cradled by grass and soft, wet dirt.

Right before I drift off, I start to worry that I somehow won't wake up in time to meet Cora.

Eight a.m. Eight a.m. Eight a.m. Eight a.m. Eight a.m. I repeat it like a drill inside my head, hoping it will somehow act as an alarm clock in the morning.

Saturday, August 16

chapter 27
Cora

I wake up to the sound of Dad yelling.

"Bethel's been declared an *evacuation zone*, Iris. Everyone is being ordered to evacuate, and I, for one, am taking myself down there and making sure each and every one of those bums loafing around there knows it and gets out."

Mom murmurs something probably intended to calm him down.

Evacuation zone, really? Does that mean the whole thing is over? Is everybody gone?

I stare at my clock. It's seven in the morning. I get up and dress quickly; definitely no white dress this time, I think, as I glare at the culprit still damp and hanging from my chair. I find a pair of denim shorts and a light orange, short-sleeved button-down shirt. I button it most of the way down and then take the bottom ends and tie them together. I quickly braid my hair and pin it into a crown around my head and slip into a pair of brown sandals.

I glance at the mirror. Definitely more hip than yesterday. And also less likely to flash a million and a half people if it rains again.

My parents' voices are coming from the kitchen. So much for baking bread. But I can at least get the eggs and see what I can scrounge up from the second pantry. I tiptoe past them and to the back door.

The rain has stopped but the ground is still wet. A basket in hand, I go into the henhouse and give my regards to *vingt-huit* through *quarante-deux* as I take their eggs.

I go back into the house. Our second pantry is a little door just off the den. It's pretty far from the kitchen and I can't even hear my parents' conversation, which makes rummaging around in there a lot calmer. I find another loaf of bread, a few more blocks of cheese, and some Macintosh apples. I also snag a couple of bags of potato chips and pretzels.

My basket is pretty full and heavy at this point; this is probably the best I can do.

By the time I emerge from the pantry and head to the front door, another voice has been added to my parents' in the kitchen. Ned.

Of course. So now I have to sneak around my dad *and* him. Added to which, I immediately conjure up the context in which I remembered him last night—right after being kissed by another boy—and I just feel deeply and utterly embarrassed for myself.

But there isn't much time for wallowing in self-pity.

The kitchen door is straight across from the front one. Of course, I could just sneak out the back door again, but then I'll never hear the end of it from my dad for leaving without saying good-bye.

There's only one way to do this and it won't be graceful.

I square my shoulders and, quickly and quietly as I can, sprint to the front door. I open the screen door gently, step outside, then yell, in one breath, "Byeseeyoualllater."

I slam the door and walk as fast as I can without looking like I'm running for cover.

"Cora," I hear both my dad and Ned call out in unison.

If they say anything else, I don't hear it. I've "walked" all the way to the end of our street and turned the corner in less than thirty seconds.

chapter 28
Michael

It turns out I don't need my internal alarm clock after all. I get woken up by trumpet.

I blink and sit up, bleary-eyed, and massage the crick in my neck as I look up to the stage.

Sure enough, a guy up there is playing a trumpet, and standing next to him is Hugh Romney. He's the leader of the Hog Farm, sort of big in the underground hippie culture, and I heard they were going to be responsible for the food here. Hugh is wearing a sleeveless white jumpsuit and a huge straw cowboy hat. He grins widely.

"What we have in mind is breakfast in bed for four hundred thousand," he says to wild applause. He tells us to hang tight, that food is coming. "And if you've got food, feed other people," he says before pointing to the guy on trumpet and asking him to play the mess call.

I stand up and stretch out as people start to stir all around me. I look down to the spot I picked as my bed for the night. It looks as if the ground and I have gone all the way together. Swirls of wet dirt peak and valley, with a deep vortex right in the area where my crotch would have been.

What the hell did I dream about last night?

And that's when I think to look down at myself and see that, obviously, my pants and shirt and arms are covered with mud. I feel really self-conscious about it for all of five seconds before I take a glance at everyone around me.

Overnight, everyone's vibrant clothes have turned a familiar shade of brown. I'll fit right in.

I squelch slowly around the field. In the distance, I see a small group of people standing on one leg in unison, their palms touching in front of them like they are in prayer. Amanda does yoga sometimes so I vaguely recognize the pose. A man in front is clearly leading the group, slowly guiding everyone into more elaborate bends and twists.

"Here you are!" a bright voice from next to me says, and I turn around to a small Dixie cup getting shoved into my hand. I look at the freckle-faced girl who has handed it to me. "Muesli and water. Eat up!" she says, before moving on to hand a cup to my neighbor.

I bring the cup to my mouth before I remember my feast from the night before. It's probably a pretty solid bet that most of the people here haven't been as lucky as I have. I bring the cup back down and, remembering Hugh's words, look for a suitable beneficiary. I finally come upon a shirtless young boy of two or three with a mop of wild, curly hair, running around in a circle, yelling raucously at the top of his lungs. I don't have to look far to find the couple staring at him dotingly, as if he's just sung "I Want to Hold Your Hand" on *The Ed Sullivan Show*.

I present the cup to them. "Muesli and water?" I ask.

"Oh! Thank you! That would be great," the woman says, taking it. "Come here, Rudy," she calls out to the boy, who runs over in a flail of limbs and primal screams.

I wisely get out of his way.

It takes me a little while to find someone with a discernible watch but when I finally do, I discover it is eight thirty. *Time to make my way over to the medical tent*, I think, and I can't help whistling a little as I do.

chapter 29
Cora

The field I cut through to get to work is a real mess. A lot of
the grass is turned up and it's obvious quite a few people have
spent the night there. Some of them are still milling about,
hanging out before the concert begins. I think about starting
to hand out food from my basket, but then decide against it.
I'll wait for Michael; it's something we can do together.

An enormous noise comes from behind me and I whip
around just in time to see a motorcycle making its way across
the field. Three people are on it, whooping up a storm. "We
made it! We're here!" I hear one of them yell, and I can't
help but smile as the bike zips past me, kicking up mud as it
goes. I can just imagine them weaving through traffic, taking
whatever back roads they can, just to get here.

This morning, I brought the portable radio out with me
to the henhouse and heard them talking about the festival:

how the Thruway is closed down and, as my dad said, they briefly considered evacuating Bethel entirely. National radio is talking about *my town*; they even had a reporter "on the scene." Never before has my hometown been anything close to "the scene," and now here it is: the center of the country's attention for one brief, shining moment. Wild.

As I near one of Mr. Yasgur's big red barns, I see one of his sons outside, driving a wooden sign into the ground. It says FREE WATER and people are already lined up for it. I can see Mr. Yasgur himself in his button-down shirt and thick, black, square-framed glasses handing out paper cups of water and milk. He's the last person on earth you'd think would be up for hosting a whole bunch of hippies. The world is a weird and wonderful place.

I quicken my pace, the picnic basket swinging heavily beside me, eager to go and help out my fellow man myself.

I walk past the nonexistent gates and approach the yellow medical tents with caution. I don't want Anna or one of the other nurses to see me, just in case they accidentally suck me into work.

My watch says five to nine, so I hang around behind my tent for a while, my eyes scanning the area for a tall, blond boy.

But ten minutes pass, and then fifteen, and nothing. I wonder if we are standing on opposite sides of the tent, so I circle it in a wide berth, looking carefully into every face I come across.

Finally, I start wondering if he won't show. Maybe that kiss has thrown him off too. It admittedly wasn't my best and it's not like I was too encouraging, right? I frown. *Well, that's a bummer,* I think, looking down forlornly at my picnic basket.

"Cora!" I hear and turn around immediately with a smile, recognizing Michael's voice.

But he's not there. I scrunch my face in confusion before a brown hand reaches out and touches my arm gently.

I look at its owner and immediately laugh.

The mud-speckled person who's grinning at me has nary a blond hair in sight.

chapter 30
Michael

Cora looks different with the clothes she's wearing today and her hair put up. She suddenly looks a little like all the other girls here. I'm not sure how much I like it.

But it's good to see her.

"I brought provisions," she says, pointing to her picnic basket. "I thought we could hand them out together."

"Wow," I say, peeking into the basket. It's packed to the brim. "I heard a rumor that the National Guard was coming in with food or something too. But who needs them when Woodstock has got you?" I shake my head in admiration.

"Well, you get first pick." She holds out the basket to me.

I think about refusing again but, to tell the truth, I'm a little hungry. I finally settle for taking an apple.

"Thanks," I say. "Let's go over by the lake. I thought I saw a bunch of families over there."

"Whoa," she exclaims as we near the water. "There are so many people. How on earth are we going to pick and choose who to give the food to?"

"Um . . . ," I start, scanning the crowd. "How about . . . we pick the people who are wearing orange. Like you."

"What would that make us? Orangists?"

"You've found me out." I hang my head in shame. "My deepest, darkest secret. Good call on your shirt color, by the way. Otherwise, I don't know if I could've been seen with you."

"Lucky me. Ah, there's one now." She points to a middle-aged man wearing an orange bandanna.

We start toward him.

"So . . . ," I say, taking a bite of the apple. "Tell me about yourself."

She laughs. "What do you want to know?"

"Um, I'll settle for *your* deepest, darkest secret. And, maybe your shoe size." She laughs again. It's looking to be a good day for me, charm-wise. Which is great; I only seem to have about five of them a year.

"Six and a half," she says. "You?" We reach the man, and she bends down and opens up her picnic basket. "Sir, some food?"

The man's face lights up. "For me?" he asks.

"Absolutely," she says. "Take what you need. Except the eggs. They aren't cooked yet. I have to get those over to the food stands."

He reaches in and comes up with a couple of slices of bread, thanking her profusely.

"Of course," she says with a smile before turning back to me.

"You sure you want to just open up the basket for people? What if someone takes everything?" I ask.

"Well, if they're wearing orange," she whispers, "I trust them."

"Good point," I answer as we scan the field some more. "Two o'clock. Orange skirt."

She nods and we head in that direction.

"So?" she asks.

"What?"

"What's *your* shoe size?"

"Oh, nuh-uh," I counter. "You answer all my questions first and then I'll answer yours."

"Oh, is that how it works?"

"Absolutely. What, you never played this game before?"

"I have led a deprived life in my little farm town," she says, putting on a drawl.

"It's okay. I will show you the way of the cosmopolitan world. And as payment . . . your deepest, darkest secret." I stop and hold out my hand, my palm open as if waiting to receive my set price.

"Well . . . ," Cora says, a line forming between her eyebrows as she stares down at my hand. "The truth is that I would like to be a . . . nurse. There. I said it!" She looks up into my eyes then, brazen.

"What?" I sputter. "That is unexpected. And shocking."

"Isn't it just?" she says before walking over to the girl in the orange skirt and opening up her picnic basket. Once she's a few apples and hunks of cheese lighter, she comes back.

"I just never expected this from you, Cora."

"I know."

"I mean, you? A liar?"

"Hey!" Cora objects.

"Biggest, darkest secret, my ass," I say. "Pathetic."

"All right. Well, since we're on my territory, we're going to play the Bethel version of this game. In which you spill your guts in front of me, right here, right now."

"I am an open book," I say. "Ask me anything and I swear I will not lie."

"Okay. What is *your* shoe size?"

"Ten."

"And which of your teachers did you have a crush on?"

"Ms. Abernathy," I say without any hesitation. "Tenth-grade science. Great legs."

"And what's your favorite thing in the whole wide world?"

"Music," I answer, throwing my apple core on the ground for emphasis. "Glorious music."

"What do you play?"

"Play?" I ask.

"Yeah. Any instruments? Drums? The guitar?"

"Oh," I say. "No, I don't play anything."

"Why not?" she asks.

I shrug. "I don't know. I just . . . appreciate it, I guess. The music."

"Oh," Cora says.

Suddenly our playful banter has grown uncomfortable and I know exactly why. She has managed to hit at the one big problem of being me.

I chuckle. "See, the thing is, you're the type of person who knows exactly what she wants to be. And it's something amazing and useful. And that's awesome. But I'm the type of person who is completely useless. A lazy good-for-nothing, as they would say." I try to lighten the mood with some good old-fashioned self-deprecation.

But she's not having it. "Why do you say that?" she asks. She stops walking and looks up at me, forcing me to stop too.

"Oh, you know." I shrug helplessly. "It's like I don't want to go to college. And I don't want to go fight. I don't know what I want."

Cora says, "You're seventeen. I'm not so sure you're supposed to know what you want."

"Eighteen, actually."

"Oh, well, in that case. What *is* your life plan, you hippie bum?"

I laugh. "Handing out food to people wearing orange. Obviously." I take the picnic basket from her. It's heavy and I feel a little bad that I didn't think to take it from her earlier.

I head toward a guy with an orange-enough tie-dyed shirt and open up the basket for him.

"How much?" he asks suspiciously.

"What?" I ask.

"How much do you want for it?"

"Nothing," I respond. "It's all free."

His eyes widen. "Really? Oh, thanks so much, man. This is fantastic," he says as he does what I was worried about earlier and takes an entire loaf of bread and four apples.

"Man, you wouldn't believe it. There was some old guy walking around here charging a dollar for water. Can you imagine paying one whole dollar for water?!"

"That's awful," Cora says. "But, hey, if you walk over that way, you'll see a big red barn. They're handing out free water and milk over there."

"Serious?" he asks.

Cora nods.

"You guys are far out, man. The absolute best. And here I was thinking this whole shindig was going to the dogs. An hour ago there was the guy with the water, and then there was another old guy telling us we'd all have to evacuate. It was crazy."

Cora frowns. "Wait, really? What did he look like?"

"Who?" the guy asks.

"The man who said you might have to evacuate."

"Oh, I don't know," he says. "He had, like, white hair and glasses."

"Ah, okay." She looks visibly relieved.

After the guy leaves, I have to ask her. "Who did you think it was?"

She takes a breath, and I say "Your dad?" at the same time that she says "My dad."

Cora laughs. "He made quite an impression last night, huh?"

"After a fashion," I admit. "I can only thank the god of Woodstock—that's Jimi Hendrix by the way—he didn't see me."

"Jimi Hendrix, huh?"

I close my eyes and bow my head in reverence. "Naturally. The one and only."

"Can't say I ever listened to him," she says in a shockingly casual way.

My eyes pop open. "Wait. What?! That's like saying you've lived on earth and haven't felt the sun. Or swum in the ocean. That's like you've never eaten a Hershey's bar. His playing, man . . . it'll just transport you. It's like he's one with his instrument and it's all coming from some great beyond where there's only pure inspiration and creativity. He's like a vessel to another land of unsullied, unadulterated . . ." I can't even think of the word, so I just take my air guitar and strike a pose with a look of intense triumph on my face.

Cora smiles. "I see. Well, that does sound pretty cool."

"Pretty cool? No, no, no. Jimi is not pretty cool. Jimi is the. Man. Period."

"The funny thing is, you know what I'm really hearing here?" Cora asks.

"What?"

"Maybe it's time you picked up a guitar of your own."

chapter 31
Cora

It's not long before all that's left in the basket are the eggs that I said I would deliver to the food tents. It turns out that the purple tents at the top of the hill are still closed down, but Michael leads me to a blue tent a little farther afield than our medical tents. As we make our way over to them, I think about Michael asking me my deepest, darkest secret. He said I'd lied.

He's right.

I almost told him the truth: about wanting to be a doctor. He probably wouldn't have immediately changed the subject. He doesn't have Ned's medical knowledge or his ambitions to make me feel silly about it. But something held me back and now I'm sorry. After all, when else does one get to spill her deepest secret to a handsome stranger she'll never see again after this weekend?

We find the people with the silk-screened flying pig bandannas—the Hog Farm people, Michael tells me. I find this pretty hilarious considering I know actual people who run hog farms and they look nothing like these commune folks. But they gladly take the eggs off our hands. They even give us a red bandanna each for our troubles. Michael immediately ties his around his long, shaggy hair. Before today, I wouldn't have thought I'd find a guy in a headband dreamy but, well, let's just say this festival is really opening up my horizons.

"What are you going to do with yours?" Michael asks me.

I consider for a moment, before finally deciding to tie it around my wrist.

"Allow me." Michael swoops in as soon as I fumble with tying the knot, and gently wraps the fabric around my wrist and ties it into an impressive-looking bind. "Boy Scouts?" I ask.

He turns the fabric around so that the flying pig is proudly displayed right side up. "Nine years." He grins. "And the only reason I didn't become an Eagle Scout is because I got too lazy to do the big project that's required."

"Shame," I say. "I love a man in uniform." I wink at him and spy the toothless guy with the cowboy hat I saw yesterday, now giving me a big thumbs-up and a grin. Which, for some reason, makes me blush. "Who's that? Do you know?" I ask to try to divert attention from my possible awkward reply.

Michael looks over at him. "Oh, sure. That's Hugh Romney. He's the Hog Farm leader." I smile politely at Hugh and he tips his hat to me before his attention gets called back to the small army of helpful hippies he's clearly marshaling.

It's already five to eleven by the time we get back to my medical tent. I take out the candy striper apron that's at the very bottom of the now empty picnic basket and tie it on. It matches my new wrist adornment pretty perfectly. Already, the tent is busy, and I can hear a couple of freak-outs happening on the inside.

"Hi, Cora," Anna says as she walks out of the tent to help someone hobble inside.

"Hi," I say to her. She smiles at Michael and me as she goes back inside.

"Thanks for helping out," I say to him.

"Thanks for the apple. And all the food last night."

"Of course."

There's an awkward moment of silence that I finally break with a very smooth "Well . . ."

"Would you be able to come see the concert with me some more today?"

"Oh . . . ," I say. "Well, I have to work."

"Right," Michael says. "Maybe during your lunch break?"

"Um . . . I'm not sure. It seems busy. . . ."

"She has a lunch break at one," Anna says as she swishes by me again, this time to help one of the other nurses, who is carrying a tray of paper cups filled with water. "And we have extra medical personnel today so no problem if she's gone for an hour."

I blush as Anna whizzes back into the tent. The woman

gets too much pleasure out of my nonexistent love life. Being in your forties must be really boring.

Michael just looks excited, though. "So, I'll meet you here at one, then?" he asks.

"Okay," I say, not sure what excuse I could possibly give now. Although why I would even want to give an excuse, I honestly have no idea. Sometimes, it's really confusing being me.

"Okay," he says, and stands there some more.

I'm worried he'll kiss me again and I don't think I can handle the whirlpool of crazy that brought on the night before. So I give him what I think is a friendly pat on the shoulder and say, "See you later, then," before I lift the tent flap and go inside.

It's busy but Anna is right: There's a noticeable increase in the doctors and nurses milling about.

"Cute," Anna says to me, as I find a corner to stash my picnic basket. "Looks a little like one of these rock star guys." She hands me some Band-Aids and points me in the direction of two mud-spattered girls with cuts on their legs.

"I thought you wanted me and Ned to get back together," I shoot back.

Anna shrugs. "Nothing wrong with a little friendly competition to get a man to come to his senses." Then she pauses. "Do *you* want you and Ned to get back together?"

"No idea," I mumble before walking over to my new patients.

While I clean up their wounds, the girls tell me about an

epic dance party in the mud that apparently led to an equally epic tumble. But it sounds like a few scratches here and there were worth the fun.

"We really need to make an announcement about the brown acid," I hear from behind me. A guy with dark, curly hair—one of the newer personnel—is flipping through our charts. "There seem to be a lot of incidents with it here."

"Oooh, yeah. I heard about that," one of my patients says, and I turn back around to her. "Someone told me it was poison. Like some guy took it last night and then this morning was having convulsions. He almost died!"

"Really?" her friend asks. And then, after a moment, "What did we take?"

"Shrooms. Totally different. We'll be fine."

It's only as I put on the final Band-Aid that I let their words really sink in. As soon as I'm done, I run over to the charts and flip through them too until I find the page with Michael's name on it.

There, in Anna's neat penmanship: "tripping out/brown acid."

chapter 32
Michael

I am going to die.

I don't remember much about yesterday morning, but that thin piece of film on Evan's palm, I can suddenly see the color plain as day. The same color as the dirt.

My mind starts to race. Sure, the guy who just told his friend he heard the brown stuff is poison doesn't look like the world's foremost medical expert.

But I am definitely sweating now. In a way that seems unhealthy, like I have a fever. And then my right temple starts to throb against my new Hog Farm insignia. Is it possible for my head to just combust, splattering my brains all over the fields of Woodstock?

I feel nauseous. It's going to happen today. I'll leave my parents an orphan. Wait . . . no, that's not how that works. But still, as an only child, I'll leave my mother childless. She will die of grief. Maybe my father will notice and be upset too.

I feel something on my shoulder and I jump a mile. I turn around, bewildered.

It's Cora.

"Whoa. It's okay. Just me," she says.

I immediately reach out and hug her tightly, partially in relief at seeing her and partially because I don't want to miss the opportunity in case my skull explodes at any moment.

About two seconds later, I feel pretty awkward about it. Especially when I let go and see that I've left streaks of mud all over her orange shirt.

"Sorry!" I say. "It's just . . . I heard . . . the acid . . ." I can't seem to get my thoughts together. Surely another precursor to croaking.

"Brown tab?" She finishes my thought.

I nod. Oh, God. She knows I'm going to die and she came out here to tell me in person. She's even holding my hand to soften the blow.

"You'll be . . . ," she starts, and I find that I'm holding my breath. "Fine."

I stare at her. "What? Really?"

Cora nods. "Yeah. I mean you got the worst of it yesterday. I checked with Anna, too. She said you might have some slight repercussions today, but nothing dire."

The pain in my temple is already starting to subside.

"But just in case," she continues, "I think I'll stay with you today."

"Really?" I say, taken aback. "What about work?"

"Well, technically, I'm a volunteer. And besides, it'll still be work being with you."

I'm still in a state of shock from my reprieve from death and don't smile at the joke, but she does.

"It's okay. Anna said she won't need me, especially when she saw how worried I was about you. And anyway, she wants me to enjoy the concert. How often does a person have this in her backyard?"

She sweeps her left hand out in front of her, her right one still holding on to mine.

"Come on," she says, as she leads me toward the stage.

chapter 33
Cora

"Cora, wait up!"

We haven't gotten very far toward the stage when I turn around to see my brother and his friend Laurie jogging up to us. They are both carrying their antiwar signs. Wes has a new one, I see. Behind them are Adam and Peter, who are huddled together, discussing something.

"Hi, Cora," Laurie says to me with a big smile.

"Hi," I say.

"Who's this?" she asks, pointing at Michael.

It's only then that I realize I'm holding Michael's hand, right about the same time my twin brother does. He looks Michael up and down.

I drop his hand as nonchalantly as I can, using mine to wave gallantly to him instead. "Michael, Laurie. Laurie, Michael. And that's Adam and Peter." I needlessly point to the two boys who are deeply in the middle of an argument and not paying us the slightest mind.

Laurie shakes his hand. "How do you do?"

Wes turns to me. "You spent all day yesterday roaming this place, right?" he asks, casting a suspicious glance at Michael, who has somehow become immediately absorbed in conversation with Laurie.

"What makes you say that?" I ask. I'm not about to give anything away.

"Cora, the whole neighborhood could hear Dad last night."

I grimace. "Yeah, I guess. What of it? And just when did *you* get home last night, anyway?"

"Jeez. Calm down." He puts his hands up in the air in a placating gesture.

Now I genuinely want to know, though. "I'm serious, Wes. When did you get home last night? And did Dad say anything to you?" My bet is on no.

Wes rolls his eyes. "Maybe like half an hour before you," he finally says. "And no, he didn't. But don't you think Dad has enough to criticize me about without the curfew bit?"

I soften a little because he's right. Seeing my face concede, he gets a mischievous gleam in his eye and looks over to where Michael and Laurie are talking to each other. "But I'm beginning to think thou dost protest too much. What's going on with Tall, Blond, and Muddy here?"

"Nothing," I say. "Can you maybe get your own love life and stay out of mine?"

"Aha! You said 'love life'!" He stares critically at Michael again. "Really? That guy? Isn't he like a drugged-out hippie?"

"You know who you sound like, right?" I ask, ready to pounce.

"Okay, okay. Just . . . be careful."

I roll my eyes. "You too. Watch out for splinters."

I look at his sign, which today reads DIE AT 18 BUT VOTE AT 21. DO YOU SEE A PROBLEM HERE?

"Wordy," I say.

"But it makes a good point."

"True," I say.

"Laurie came up with it," he says just as Laurie gives a loud guffaw. I look to see both her and Michael doubled over in laughter.

I frown. I don't like this. Especially since blond-haired, blue-eyed Laurie looks a little like Michael's girlfriend.

Right. His *girlfriend.*

On second thought, this is a good reminder for me that he has one. And I should keep myself to myself. No more hand holding, or hugging, or weird pecks. Thank you, Laurie.

"Anyway, I think Mark would approve," Wes says, looking over at his sign again.

I reach out and lightly touch his sign then, like it's somehow a connection to my absent older brother. "Your letter from him was bad too?" I ask, although it's not really a question.

Wes shakes his head. "We got to get him out of there," he mutters.

If only, I think.

"Oh, man. Look at that." Michael's voice pulls me out of

my thoughts. I look up to see him pointing toward a bunch of people who are pushing a Volkswagen van up a steep hill—everything, naturally, the color of mud. They get a few inches of the way up, about five feet from the crest, before the car starts rolling back down again. Then I hear a couple of the girls scream as they duck out of the way of the free-flying vehicle. Once the van has made its way back to the bottom, they jog back down there and try again.

"What's the van doing on the field in the first place?" Wes asks with just a touch of incredulity, and I can't help smiling to myself. One day, he'll see just how uncanny his resemblance to our dad really is.

Adam and Peter stop their conversation and we all watch the saga of the van unfold, as more and more people nearby rush to help. Now there are five people pushing. And then, once it rolls down again, six. At that moment, I'm sure we're all equating it to something or other in our lives, the futile struggle, the resistance to inevitable failure.

Me? I go a bit more of a literal route. The van makes me think of the back of Ned's truck. In early March, it was too cold to be in the barn, which would have offered more room.

Oh, fine, there's some metaphor in there, too. Futile struggles and last-ditch efforts and all that. Only I was a girl in love, and a girl in love often can't see when something has stalled for good. She'd rather spend all her energy trying to move a large hunk of metal up a mountain than face the truth. Because truth is the enemy of hope.

I am, thankfully, distracted from my thoughts by the loud

noise of a helicopter flying low right over us. It's green with the US Army's logo emblazoned on its door.

"What are they doing here?" Wes asks breathlessly as we all stare up at it.

It hovers lower and lower. And then, right in front of our eyes, a package falls from it.

"Oh my God. Are they gassing us?" Adam asks.

"No, man!" We turn around to see a prematurely balding guy with a compensatory long beard. "They're *feeding* us. The US Army is bringing us food."

"No. Way," Wes says, but from where we are, we can see the Hog Farm folks gathering around whatever was dropped from the helicopter, their bright red strips of fabric flying in the wind from the rotating blades.

My brother and his friends all hold their signs by their sides now. Right about where their jaws are.

chapter 34
Michael

After Cora's brother and his friends go off to further investigate the army helicopter, I excuse myself for a few minutes. I really need to take a leak and there are some bushes that are calling my name. We're also by the lake again and I think it might be nice to get some of the mud off, at least from my face.

Kneeling down near the water, I'm hit with a strong smell of cow shit. I see myself make a face in my reflection, and move over a little before splashing my face and arms. The water is cold but refreshing and it washes off most of the mud. I'm not sure if it's drinkable, but then I spy a bunch of others happily lapping up handfuls. I shrug and do the same. If I can survive poisonous brown acid, surely a little farm-town water can't hurt me.

"I'm a new man!" I say as I present myself to Cora.

"Sparkling clean," she says after giving me a once-over.

"Absolutely. If you think about it, this could totally be a brown suit." I look down at my still-spackled threads. "I could be a banker in these clothes."

"You are the specimen of trust and responsibility."

"Thank you." As we walk toward the stage, the smell of fertilizer hits my nose again and I mention something about it to Cora.

"Yeah, that happens at a farm," she said. "Of course, this isn't just cow manure."

"What do you mean?" I ask. "Like, other animals?"

"Yeah," she laughs. "The bipedal kind."

It finally dawns on me what she's saying and I look around at the spread of humanity before us. "Ugh. Really?"

"'Fraid so," she says. "There's no way a couple hundred thousand people can hold it in for a few days, you know."

All I know is that I've managed to so far and I hope I won't be adding to the beautification of Bethel's farmlands myself.

"So we're walking around in crap. And that doesn't bother you?" I ask.

"When you work at a hospital, you see a lot of crap. In many senses of the word," she says.

"You are an unusual girl."

The rest of my words are cut off by a loud chopping sound and a strong gust of wind. I look up to see that we are right by a helicopter that's about to touch down. No US Army writing on this one.

I immediately perk up.

"I heard that's how the artists are getting here!" I say to

Cora, who only mouths the word "What?" to me. I end up having to shout in her ear that I heard they are staying at some hotel nearby and are being shuttled back and forth this way.

By this point, the helicopter's door has opened.

"Let's get closer!" I yell. "I want to see if we can see anybody."

She nods and follows me. I am staring so intently at the chopper that I don't even see the burly guy who has slipped right in front of me. I almost step on the toe of his boot.

"Man, where do you think you're going?" he asks.

I look up at him and start to apologize. "Oh, sorry . . ." is all I get out, before I feel a hand clap my back.

"Roger?" I turn around to see a man in a suit. He has a thick moustache, dark hair, and big sunglasses. "Is that you?" He takes off his sunglasses and squints at me for a second before giving a little nod of confidence. "You're here early. How did you get here?" His sunglasses go back on.

"Ummm . . . ," I say, and realize I'm saying it in unison with the guard.

The suit turns to the burly guy then. "Hello? Don't you know who this is? Roger Daltrey. From the Who. Let him through, will you?"

I'm sure my mouth drops open and I know Cora's does. But I immediately shut it and follow the guy in the suit.

Because if someone thinks you're Roger Daltrey, you fucking go with it.

"And who are you?" I turn around to see the guard moodily interrogating Cora.

"She's with me," I say immediately, and reach out for her hand.

The suit turns around and sees us. He rolls his eyes but comes back over. "Just let them both through. Look, I'm from Polydor." He lazily points to the badge that's pinned to his lapel. Holy crap. That's Jimi's label too.

But before I can think of something even remotely coherent and/or viable to ask him about Jimi, he asks me, "Did you want to get on the copter? They're just dropping off Joe McDonald." Wow. As in Country Joe McDonald. "But it's going back to the hotel now. If you want a lift."

Dear, sweet mother of Hendrix. I swear I can hear my heart pounding in every single one of my extremities. "Do not screw this up, Michaelson," it thumps to my brain.

Which is the exact moment that I remember that Roger Daltrey is British.

"Oh, aye. Indeed. Moust get back to the 'otel. Eh?" I say.

The executive gives me a weird look.

"Just straight that way?" I ask more quietly, hoping the sound of the helicopter might mask my voice a little.

"Yeah . . . ," the executive says slowly.

I decide to skip speaking altogether this time and salute him, practically jogging to the helicopter, my hand pulling Cora along with me.

In a moment, the executive is beside me, his hand on my shoulder once again.

Oh, crap. I knew it was too good to be true. I just hope I won't get kicked out of the concert entirely.

The exec turns me around and looks into my eyes. "Hey, Rog. Just . . . straighten out a little before the show, all right? Maybe take an aspirin?" He looks at my banker's suit. "And maybe a bath?"

"Aye! Will do, sir," I say and then, in a bout of inspiration, "Roger that!"

I practically skip right onto the helicopter.

chapter 35
Cora

I can't believe I'm in a helicopter, Bethel spread out below me like a patchwork quilt. A true bird's-eye view. I wish *vingt-huit* could fly. I have a feeling she would love this.

I look over at Michael and he grins back at me, wild-eyed. Obviously, neither one of us can believe he got away with this. I chuckle, thinking about his ridiculous accent. I wonder what we are going to do when we get to the hotel. He definitely can't pull off this Roger Daltrey act forever. Even I know Daltrey is the lead singer of the Who, though, I admit, I'm a bit hazy on what he looks like exactly. Evidently, so is his record label guy.

The helicopter is following Route 17 now, which looks like a giant parking lot. Hundreds and hundreds of cars are abandoned by the side and there's no traffic going in either direction, except for a lone police motorcycle I see weaving its way through. Michael points at one of the cars and mouths, I think, the words "That's my car." I nod, having no idea which one he's really pointing out.

It's too loud in the helicopter to talk, but I have a question I'm dying to ask him once we get out.

Within twenty minutes, we are touching down again, and I laugh when I see the hotel we're being taken to. It's the Holiday Inn in Liberty. I don't know why I thought it'd be some super-fancy hotel—there aren't any nearby—but in my visions of rock-'n'-roll lodgings, this certainly wouldn't be at the top of my list.

The pilot gets out and opens the door for us, helping us both out. Michael just smiles at him and starts to walk toward the building. He's probably realized he should keep the talking to a minimum.

I catch up to him, my ears still ringing. When I feel we are far enough away from the pilot, I sidle up to him and say, "You'll have to show me a picture of Roger Daltrey sometime."

Michael blushes and turns around to look at me. I laugh and he opens his mouth as if to say something. But then, with the color still in his cheeks, his eyes darken too. And before I know what's happening, he grabs the red and white apron strings that are still tied around my waist and pulls me close. His green eyes stare into mine, the flying pig on his forehead soars toward me, and then he kisses me.

It's a completely different kiss from last night. This is a kiss from a rock god, full of passion and confidence. I'm taken aback by how much I feel it reverberate through my body, and then even more so when I find myself kissing him back.

I stumble forward a little when he finally pulls away, and he pushes his hand up tighter against my back to steady me.

He grins wickedly at me.

"Um . . . ," I say, feeling a little dizzy still. *Wow.* "So . . . are you going to miss any acts at the concert? Anyone you really want to see?"

It's a non sequitur really, but what am I going to do? Comment on the kiss? I'm still trying to wrap my head around what just happened.

"I don't think so but . . . oh, wait!" He sees a girl with a clipboard and a badge pinned to her red shirt and runs over to her.

"Excuse me, but would you happen to have the schedule of the lineup?"

"Um, sure," she says, as she flips to a page on her clipboard, and lets Michael peek over her shoulder. I see him scan the page, flip it, and then smile and nod. "Thanks very much!"

"Jimi's on last thing tomorrow night," he says when he's walked back over to me. "Which I knew. And I definitely want to be back by tonight when, um, I'm on." He grins. "And I wouldn't mind seeing Canned Heat this afternoon. And this new guy Santana is supposed to be pretty special. My cousin lives in California, and he's caught him a couple of times."

"What time?" I ask.

"Around four, I think," he says.

"Okay, so we should try to get back by then?" Though,

honestly, I'm not sure how we're going to do that.

Michael nods. "Yup."

I stare up at the nondescript, squat brick building, which suddenly looks a lot more intimidating than any Holiday Inn ever has a right to look.

"Are we going in?"

"Absolutely," Michael says, his head held high as he strolls right up to the front door and opens it gallantly for me.

I'm starting to believe that rock god really is a state of mind.

chapter 36
Michael

This is unbelievable.

First, I get mistaken for Roger freakin' Daltrey. Then, I'm feet away from entering the same building where the world's greatest musicians have been sleeping. And finally, I manage to land a scorching one on a really hot girl. I even think her knees were trembling a little when the kiss ended.

And I'm not even on anything. Who would have thought? Can this day possibly get any better?

Well, maybe if I see Jimi in the flesh, up close.

"I think we should keep a low profile," I murmur to Cora as we approach the hotel. No sense in pushing our luck.

Frankly, security seems pretty lax. No one even gives us a second look. Scanning the crowd in the lobby, I see a few older folks. A lot of them are in suits and have badges similar to the guy who let me on the helicopter, a.k.a. my new best friend.

"Now what?" Cora asks.

"Maybe we'll see someone amazing?" I say. "Let's take a stroll through the lobby." I hold on to her hand and try to channel my inner cool. If I look nonchalant, like I belong here, I think we can probably continue to get away with this.

I stroll casually from one side of the lobby to the other, keeping an eye out the whole time. If I'm honest, mostly for a telltale Afro.

At the end of the lobby is a small bar with stools and several tables and chairs scattered around. A clump of people are gathered at one end of it.

I hear the murmur of a soft-spoken voice and the sound of laughter before I see her. She's surrounded by several people laughing at her jokes, and I catch a glimpse of her tie-dyed outfit as she turns around to ash her cigarette at the bar.

I'm standing about five feet away from Janis Joplin, who has a cigarette dangling from one hand and a glass of whiskey clenched in the other.

I duck down and whisper furiously in Cora's ear. "Do you know who that is?"

She squints over at the group and after a moment says, hesitatingly, "Janis Joplin?"

"Yes!" I yell, louder than I intended. But Christ, even Cora knows who she is. This is huge.

"Come on, we're getting a drink."

I sidle up to the bar as casually as I can. The bartender looks me up and down before ambling over slowly. "Yes?" he asks.

"I'll have a beer. Two," I say quickly, indicating Cora. Janis has gotten me so flustered that I almost forgot my manners.

He cocks one eyebrow. "What sort of beer?" he asks.

"Um ..." Crap. I've been eighteen for a little over a month now, legally able to drink, but I've never actually ordered a beer at a bar before. Who needs to with Evan around?

"What's on tap?" I hear a voice behind me ask, and turn around to see Cora playing this whole nonchalant, I'm-really-much-older-than-I-look thing much better than me.

The bartender gives her a once-over too. "Budweiser and Schlitz," he says.

"We'll take one of each," she shoots back confidently.

The bartender slowly takes out two glasses and gives us one more suspicious glance before he starts to fill them.

"Man, what sort of insanity is going on out there? Are there cats slinging mud?"

I follow the source of the soft voice to catch Janis looking straight at me and my muddy clothes.

Janis Joplin is speaking *to me*. Holy fuck.

I don't respond. How the hell do you respond to Janis Joplin? I just stare at her, my mouth hanging open, unblinking. All thoughts of inner Roger Daltry–ness gone.

"Is he all right?" she asks, and I can see she has now turned to Cora.

Cora glances at me and then speaks to Janis without blinking an eye. "He's fine." She smiles. "But I would stay away from the brown tabs," she adds.

"Ah," Janis says. "Thanks for the tip, sister." She salutes us before turning back to her entourage, who are starting to gather their things.

"So . . . hey," Cora says quietly, forcing me to divert my attention away from the rock superstar for a moment. "Do you have any money for these?" She brings her face close so that she can ask me under her breath.

I look down at the two beers that are now sitting in front of us, behind which stands an impatient bartender.

"Crap," I croak out. What little money I have is in my backpack, of course. Far, far away with my lost friends.

Cora shakes her head before putting on a beaming smile and turning to the ever-more-irate-looking bartender. "Sir," she says. "I am so sorry about this. My friend thought he had his wallet with him, but . . ."

"I poured it, you buy it," the bartender says. "Those are the rules."

"Right," Cora says. "I understand, only we unfortunately don't have any cash on us. I'm really sorry."

"No exceptions," the bartender says.

"Um. Okay," Cora says. "But let's just say we don't have any money to give you. But we also didn't drink any of the beer. So then . . ."

"Then I think someone might be washing some glasses today," the bartender says with a sneer.

Panic starts to set in. I *cannot* be in the back of a hotel washing glasses while the greatest musicians in the world are playing just a handful of miles away.

"Oh, just put it on my room bill, Charlie. And stop giving them crap." Janis has poked her face between our shoulders and is staring down the bartender.

Once again, I stare at her agape, this time my mouth hanging open about three inches from her face.

Cora at least has the presence of mind to say, "Oh, wow. Thanks so much . . ."

"Just repaying the favor for the acid tip," Janis says with a wink. "See you out there." She turns around and starts following her guys back through the lobby.

I just stare in her wake, still completely mute.

"Well," Cora says as she takes both beers from underneath the bartender's hateful gaze. "Might as well enjoy these." She takes them over to one of the lobby tables and sits down.

I follow her, but not until I've watched Janis swish onto one of the hotel elevators.

Janis Joplin has just bought me a beer. I sit across from Cora and stare into the frothy glass. This has to go down as one of the most amazing drinks in the history of alcohol.

chapter 37
Cora

A couple of sips into his beer and Michael seems to have relaxed enough to form sentences again. Pretending to be a rock god, not bad. In the presence of a rock goddess, total disaster.

But once he regains some of his composure, he starts to excitedly fill me in on what exactly makes Janis so great ("Her voice. It's so raw. Like the joy and pain of existence itself is transmitting through her."). He even tells me about some of the other bands he mentioned before, like Canned Heat ("Perfect, pure blues music. Which is really the basis of rock-'n'-roll.") and Santana ("Not that anybody can beat Jimi, but my cuz says he's a worthy second. So I'm curious as all hell.").

He honestly knows more about music than anyone I've ever met. It's pretty impressive, and I tell him so.

He shrugs good-naturedly, but I can tell he's pleased. "It's not very often that I actually know more about something than someone else. Trust me. We should both enjoy this moment for the rarity that it is."

I laugh.

"What about you?" he asks, as he takes another sip from his beer. "Since you're obviously not spending time as the president of your local Doors fan club, what's your favorite thing to do? For fun?"

I consider this, not sure anyone's ever really asked me that before. Truthfully, I don't think most people who know me would think to put the word "fun" in the same sentence as "Cora." "Um . . . I like the movies?" I finally offer lamely.

"Oh, yeah? Seen any good ones lately?"

I have to rack my brain a little, because I haven't actually been to the movies since Ned and I broke up. What was the last one we saw together? Oh, right. John Wayne. His choice. "*True Grit*," I finally remember the name. "It was pretty good."

Michael nods. "I missed that one." Then his face lights up. "Oh, but have you heard of this new one, *Easy Rider*? I haven't actually gotten around to seeing it yet, but I've heard it's supposed to be amazing. Really different."

I shake my head no, starting to think that maybe I'm not *that* into movies if I can't even be bothered to go to one alone. "See? Here's another thing you actually know more about than me." I throw my hands up in the air.

He opens his mouth to say something, but then closes it again. For a wild second, I think he's about to ask me out to the movies. But then he surprises me with a different question.

"So what do you *really* like to do, Cora?" He grasps his beer glass in both hands, his head cocked, looking at me intently across it. "In your spare time?"

I eye him. "Honestly?" I ask, and he nods. "I don't really have much spare time. I'm either at school or helping out at my farm. And the rest of the time, I'm volunteering at the hospital." He's looking at me quizzically and I wonder if he's thinking about how boring that sounds. If that's the case, I might as well go all in and admit it. "But actually, I find that really fun. My work at the hospital. I just . . . love it. Does that sound completely insane?" I look down into my own beer glass, and see the strings from my candy striper apron dangling near the floor through the bottom.

"Insane? Um, no. Impressive? Hell, yes." When I look up, Michael is beaming at me.

I laugh. "You probably wouldn't say that if you actually knew what being a candy striper mostly entailed."

"Saving people from dying because of bad acid, right? I assume that's a daily task."

"Oh, yes. Happens all the time here in Bethel. Where, by the way, I think the median age is fifty," I counter.

"Old people. What is the matter with them these days?" Michael shakes his head. "Why can't they take a page from our book? Wholesome, respectful, clean-cut . . ."

I reach across the table and lightly touch his shoulder-length hair. "Very clean-cut." Then I snort, remembering something else. "Oh, right. The other fifteen percent of my spare time is spent trying to stop my father and Wes from murdering each other. Wes's hair is the latest point of contention. You know, along with their points of view on the war, and the farm, and school, and his clothes, and basically anything it's possible to have an opinion about." I've stopped touching his hair, but my hand is still hovering near his side of the table. He takes it in his.

"Is there a lot of fighting in your house?" he asks. He looks serious for a second, which is a look I don't think I've seen come across his face before.

I shrug. "Yes, sometimes. Sometimes a lot of begrudging silence. They both adore my mother, so she can usually butt in and get them to stop. Or sometimes I can . . ." I trail off. "My dad fought in both World War II and Korea and he's so proud of his time as a soldier. Mark was always the favorite anyway, but when he signed up for the army, he cemented that spot forever. My dad's brave and strong boy. And I was the only girl. So sometimes that leaves Wes a little bit adrift, you know?"

He nods solemnly. "Yeah, I kinda do. I'm an only child but I'm still somehow my dad's least favorite." He laughs, but I don't think it's very funny.

"What do you mean?" I ask, frowning.

But he shakes his head, and his goofy grin is back. "He's just not a warm and fuzzy guy, is all." Just like that, his serious moment seems to be over. Still holding my hand, he bends his head to try to read my watch. "Does that say three?" he asks.

I take my hand back to check. "Yup," I say. "I guess we should try to get back and catch some more of these bands?"

I make it a question, because I'm not entirely convinced that Michael doesn't want to tell me more about his parents.

"Definitely," he says with enthusiasm as he gets up from the table, dispelling any notion I have that he wants to stay on the subject. "Some of them are going to knock your socks off, I'm telling you." He offers his hand to help me up, but as he does, we look at each other and I know we're both hit with the same thought.

"How exactly are we going to get back?" I finally voice the concern.

"I take it hitchhiking is out?" Michael says.

"Unless you know of a way to tow about twenty thousand cars from Route 17. Or we find a car with wings."

"I got it." Michael snaps his fingers. "How about the same way we got here?" He grins as he starts to head for the hotel's front door.

I'm pretty skeptical. What are the chances that a second dope will mistake Michael for Roger Daltrey?

It turns out I'm right, of course. The helicopter is waiting just outside the hotel again, and I see Michael walk up to it with all the swagger he can muster. "G'day," he says to the guy in shades who is manning the door.

"Get lost, kid," the guy promptly replies.

"'Bout," Michael continues, trying on his accent once again, "ay'm Roger Daltrey."

"Oh, yeah? And I'm a leprechaun." The guy puts on a fairly impressive Irish accent before continuing. "Stop wasting me time now, laddie."

I can't help but laugh, and Michael walks back over to me, looking sullen.

"You gotta admit, his Irish accent was way better than yours," I tease.

"Mine was English!"

"Oh . . . ," I say, and can't help giggling.

"How far is it to the festival?" Michael asks.

"Um . . . about twenty miles," I answer.

"So . . . walking is out of the question?"

"Unless we want to get there on Sunday night," I say.

I can see a worried expression creeping into Michael's handsome features. "So how *do* we get back?" he asks. I'm sure he's thinking about Jimi.

"Didn't really think that far, did you?" I ask gently.

"No," he admits. "I guess I never really do. It's my fatal flaw, according to my mom."

I stare at the helicopter and watch as the guy in shades is relieved of his duty by a heavier-set guy. Then I look down at my red-and-white apron and am suddenly hit by an idea.

"Come with me," I say.

chapter 38
Michael

"You're *what?*" The burly helicopter pilot is looking Cora over skeptically. She doesn't bat an eye.

"Dr. Fletcher. I think you heard me the first time," she says in a curt but calm voice.

"*You're* a doctor?" He takes the cigarette out of his mouth and glances over at me incredulously, as if I'm going to back him up. I try to keep my face neutral.

"My volunteer." Cora indicates me and then snaps his attention back to her. "We've just got news of a cardiac arrest on-site, and I was told by the organizers to come to you so you could get me there as soon as possible. We're wasting valuable time here." She folds her arms across her chest and stares him down. Just a few minutes ago, I watched as she took off her apron and took her hair down out of its braids, tucking its long strands behind her ears. She stands tall and assured in front of the pilot now, looking imposing.

Twenty minutes later, we're touching down right near the main stage again and I can't help thinking that Cora is a genius.

I wait until we've disembarked and are far enough away from the pilot before turning to her. "Good thinking. She's not just a pretty face, folks."

"Why, thank you," Cora says, straightening out her trusty medical badge. "Good thing this thing doesn't actually say 'candy striper.'"

"Though really, couldn't I have been the doctor? Instead of the volunteer?"

"Doctor or Daltrey," she retorts. "You can't have both."

"I could totally be a doctor," I say, grinning.

But she's not smiling. "You weren't the one with the badge," she says softly, almost to herself. She moves a little bit away from me. She's fiddling with her hair, swiftly putting it into a long braid again.

"Hey, what's the matter?" I ask.

"Nothing," she responds flatly.

"Pretty and transparent," I say, keeping up with her quickened pace.

"What?" Now she's unfolding the candy striper apron she's been clutching.

"Your face. I can tell something's wrong."

She shrugs as she methodically puts her apron back on. "It's nothing."

I've been with Amanda long enough to know what "it's nothing" actually means. But I don't know if I should push it the way I always know for sure I should push it with Amanda so that she can yell at me for whatever is pissing her off and get it over with.

"So who's that?" Cora stops walking and points to the stage. A lean, olive-skinned guy in a leather vest is playing one hell of a guitar solo, while around him bongos, drums, a bass, and maracas retaliate.

I grin. "That should be Santana."

We watch him play for a bit, close enough to see his face clearly in the afternoon sun. His eyes are closed, and his face is scrunched up in concentration. It's like he's channeling a force from another planet to create the sounds that are coming from his strings.

And then, suddenly, whatever possesses him seems to get hold of the drummer, too, who goes into a long, complicated drum solo. The drummer looks young, with shaggy, light hair that's flying all over the place. He kind of looks like me, actually. I would give anything to switch places with him right now.

"Wow," I say. "They really are amazing."

"Yes?" Cora asks.

I nod. "This is all improvised. They're just bouncing off each other."

"What do you mean? They're not just playing a song they wrote before?"

"No, ma'am. They're just listening to each other and making it up on the spot."

"Wow," Cora says, and I can tell she's genuinely impressed.

"They're fantastic." We take advantage of our unbelievably close viewpoint for a little bit longer before someone with a staff T-shirt finally comes over and asks us what we're doing there. We are in the artist area, after all.

"Just on our way to the medical tents," Cora says, quickly pointing to her badge and then turning away before we get questioned further. I follow her.

She abruptly stops and I almost bump into her. She turns around and looks at me, a decisive gleam in her eyes. "The thing back there," she says. "The reason I was upset is . . . I actually want to be a doctor." She says it emphatically and then waits, as if for some sort of reaction from me.

"Okay . . . ," I say slowly. "That's great," I add, hoping it's the right thing to say. I don't see how it couldn't be. It genuinely *is* pretty great, and I'm sure she'd be good at it, doing something she so clearly loves.

But Cora just laughs bitterly. "Yeah. Pretty great. Unless you're anyone in the medical profession. Or my dad. Or Ned."

"What do you mean?"

"Did you see that helicopter guy's face when I said I was a doctor? He was thinking, 'A woman doctor?' You just don't see that around here so much. . . ."

I pause for a second. "Yeah, but in the end, he believed you, didn't he?"

"I guess. . . ." She looks down at her apron.

"Honestly, he was probably more thinking, 'She's too young to be a doctor. . . .'"

"That could be true," Cora admits, looking a little embarrassed.

I think back to the encounter. "But you know what? If he was thinking what you said, screw him," I say emphatically. "We live in the age of Gloria Steinem. You can be anything you want to be!"

Cora laughs. "You know Gloria Steinem?"

"Sure," I say, but leave it there. I don't need to continue and tell her that it's because there were a couple of months when Amanda would bring her up at least once a conversation.

I touch her arm. "That's what the music is saying, Cora," I say in all seriousness. "You can be anything you want to be. Anything at all."

We pause and listen to the guitar sing. It's clear as day to me; I hope she can hear it too. I think by the smile creeping across her face that she can.

chapter 39
Cora

At some point, someone hands us each a wrapped sandwich, telling us it's what the military has dropped off. It's been a long time since we ate, unless you count the handful of peanuts I saw Michael sneak at the hotel bar.

The sandwich is bologna on two pieces of white bread, with just a dab of mustard. Michael claims it's one of the best meals he's ever had. I'm starting to suspect he might be feeling that way about everything he's eaten here, no matter what random thing it's been. I wonder if the sound track has anything to do with it. Or the fact that he is half starved most of the time.

The girl who gives us the sandwiches tells us there's some drinkable water on one side of the lake, and Michael suggests we go to it.

The girl says to look for the sign, and I laugh when I finally see it.

NO

SOAPING

SHITTING

PISSING

SWIMMING

ETC.

IN THE

DRINKING

WATER

(OR YOU MITE

COME DOWN

WITH THE SHITS)

TRY FURTHER

——>

"Lovely poem," Michael says as he walks to the edge of the water and scoops some up with his hands.

"Very poignant," I agree, and follow suit.

After he's gotten his fill, I watch him go back to the sign and read it again thoughtfully.

"Come on," he says mysteriously as he goes in the direction of the sign's arrow.

We follow a dense tree line and then turn the corner where I know the lake expands out.

Only I've never seen the lake like this before, filled with splashing, writhing, bathing, laughing flesh. There are naked men, women, and children scattered in all parts of the water, washing off mud from their bodies and hair. There's even a familiar-looking redheaded guy who is scrubbing a sheep. He passes his soap off to a father and son once he's done.

"I think I could use a bath, actually," I hear Michael say.

When I turn to him, he has already taken off his shirt and is unbuttoning his pants.

"Oh!" I exclaim, more breathlessly than I should, considering I work in a hospital. I turn away. Within moments, he's in my sight line again, running into the lake, just miles of pale flesh stretched across his lanky body. This time, I can't help but peek.

When he's a few feet in, he immerses his whole body, head too, eventually coming back up with a grin.

"Come on, Cora!" he yells back to me. "It's amazing in here."

A beautiful naked girl hands him something and he nods in appreciation. She swims away and I squint at him before realizing she's given him a bar of soap. He is now scrubbing himself vigorously with it.

He grins at me and yells out again. "Come on!"

"I can shower at home, Michael," I yell back.

"Yes. You can," he says simply, and then holds out the bar of soap in offering.

I stare at him and the smiling faces all around him. Of course I can shower at home. But when else will I ever have the opportunity to bathe in the middle of Filippini Pond with fifty other people my age all smiling and swaying to the live music that's blasting from behind us?

I get an idea and scan the area behind me, quickly finding

what I'm looking for. I walk over to a shirtless guy wearing countless love beads around his neck.

"Could you spare a hit?" I ask, pointing to the glass pipe in his hand.

"Of course," he replies, and generously offers it to me.

Suddenly, I feel a little shy. "Um, could you show me how?" I may know the vernacular, especially after the past few days of hanging around in my tent, but I have never actually done this before. He smiles, but not really in a patronizing way. Taking his lighter, he puts a flame to one end of the pipe, then shows me how I have to hold my finger down on a small hole while I inhale. "Hold your breath for a few seconds before you exhale," he instructs.

I do as he says. It burns my throat as the smoke fills up my mouth, and I cough it all back out almost immediately. He tells me to try one more time. "Breathe in a little slower," he advises.

It stings a little less this time and I do manage to hold my breath for a few seconds before I let the smoke out. "Thank you," I say with a small cough and a smile. I give the pipe back to him and make my way to the edge of the lake again.

And then, before I can talk myself out of it, I strip down to my bra and panties and jump in.

chapter 40
Michael

Is it possible to find a corner of a lake? That's where Cora and I seem to be. I suppose that there must still be people around us, but when I reach over to touch her neck and pull her close, it's like a magic trick. They all disappear. When we kiss again, there is nothing but me, her, and the water reflecting a cloudy sky and a sinking sun.

Soulful guitar riffs drift in, as if timed to all the raw emotion I'm feeling, like a movie sound track. At one point, Cora asks me who's playing, and I tell her it's Canned Heat at last.

"At last," she repeats with a smile. "I can't wait to see exactly how big your eyes get once Jimi is finally onstage."

Just the thought of that fills me with so much electric anticipation that I have to lean over and kiss her again. This time I let my hand drift over to her bare back. The combination of her skin and the water is intoxicating, like layered softness.

I think I might burst from how much I want her, and I reluctantly pull myself away a little in case she can actually feel my desire. I don't know how she would feel about it, and I'm not ready to break the magic of the moment yet. Even for the sake of my own horniness.

I take a breath and look around, trying to bring some of the other people surrounding us into focus to calm myself down. A few feet behind us, there are two guys in a rowboat singing "Row, Row, Row Your Boat" in a round. Farther away, near the shoreline, my sight line is filled with bushels of pubic hair, skimming the surface of the water like water lilies. I see a cornucopia of tan lines, nipples of all sizes and colors, even a couple of interesting tattoos that are obviously not meant for strangers' eyes. This isn't helping much in terms of calming me down.

I suppose all those people can see me, too.

And yet, no one is watching.

Screw it. There's no point in not turning my attention back to Cora and just letting whatever happens happen.

It begins to rain again, gently at first and then a bit harder. All around us, the water plops as it's hit with itself, the line between lake and sky becoming hazy. It's like being in a bath and a shower at the same time. Cora laughs, holding her hand out to catch some raindrops and then letting them fall through her fingers into the water. *Plop.*

A piece of her hair has come undone from its braid and it trails behind her in the lake, like a silky eel.

I reach over and lift it, watching the wet, dark strands make patterns on my palm.

"It's so beautiful," I say. Then I look right at her and drink her in: her deep brown eyes and small nose; her wide lips; the slope of her shoulders, which only draws my eye downward to take in the rest of her curves, which she has, unfortunately, kept shrouded beneath the water. The red Hog Farm fabric is still around her wrist, sodden and trailing in the water like a red flag, a claim.

"*You* are so beautiful," I say, a little choked up at how true it is. Especially here, surrounded by water and music. I think that this has to be the most romantic moment of my life. Also the most erotic.

She stares back at me for an instant and I'm sure she feels the same.

Until she starts to giggle uncontrollably.

I'm startled, but I decide to laugh awkwardly with her.

"I'm sorry," she says through her laughs. "I don't know why, but this whole thing is hilarious, right?"

Um . . . no. Not the word I would use, but I just nod.

She lifts up her hand again and looks at it. "I'm getting all pruney. Time to go back to the concert, right?"

She doesn't even let me reply before she starts swimming away.

"Wait," I call out weakly.

But she doesn't and I have no choice but to swim after her, wondering what I said wrong.

chapter 41
Cora

I'm not a virgin. There. I said it.

I don't want to hear that I'm beautiful. I really don't. That's how the mess with Ned started.

It wasn't a mess at first. It was lovely and full of a raw intensity I'd never experienced before, finally a physical manifestation of the swirl of emotions I felt for him from the start. It made me feel new and grown-up, like I'd crossed a threshold.

We did it three times. The third time was the best. By then, we had figured out exactly how to move around in the car so that neither of us was being poked by the stick shift. And we were beginning to figure out how to move around each other, which areas of our bodies wanted most to be touched, the little things that made one or the other of us breathless.

And then two weeks later, it was all over.

To tell you the truth, I don't really regret not being a virgin. Things are different on this side of the threshold, and I can't ever go back, but I feel it's where I'm meant to be now. I just regret the emptiness and ache that appeared when he left, and I can't help but wonder whether I would have felt it so keenly if we hadn't gone there. I'll never know.

I finally emerge from the lake, and find my clothes magically exactly where I left them. My dad can grumble all he wants about the hippies, but they're definitely not thieves. It's stopped raining again, but my shorts, which are on top, are pretty sodden. I change into them quickly anyway and then my orange shirt, which turns into a burnt sienna as I drip all over it. But the candy striper apron I don't put on. There's too much of Ned in my head and heart at the moment, and I don't need to wear a reminder, too. I fold it and carry it over my arm.

I turn around and wait for Michael, plastering a pleasant smile on my face, the kind that pretends that nothing weird just happened.

I see a shy, perplexed smile in return. Poor boy. It's not his fault that he's caught me at such a bewildering point in my life.

"Alas, no towels," I say, and indicate my sopping wet clothes.

He nods and finds his clothes just a few feet from mine. He puts them on slowly, his back turned to me, so that I can see the drops of water that cling to his shoulders, a few of them magnifying the smattering of freckles on his back. And yes, I'm looking intently at his back so that I can't focus on his bare ass.

He finally turns around as he puts his shirt back on, and looks at me silently.

"Should we go by the stage?" I cut through the quiet. "I feel like we haven't seen much of the concert at all today."

Michael doesn't respond and I'm worried this isn't patched up like it's meant to be. So I take his hand and smile at him one more time. Then I walk ahead so that I can lead the way. And not have to look into those confused green eyes again just yet.

chapter 42
Michael

I'm a virgin. Fine. I said it. It's awful.

And it gets even worse. Ready for it? I've been with Amanda for seven months at this point. That's right, Miss "Free-Spirited" (her words, not mine) is an ice queen when it comes to sex. Seven months of staring at those perfect tits, almost always under some sort of frustrating piece of clothing, and she won't let me get past second base. Okay, fine. Third once. But for her, not for me. Which, I admit, was still enjoyable but definitely NOT THE SAME.

In case you haven't figured this out by now, Amanda isn't the return-the-favor type when it comes to anything.

Sometimes I think I really don't understand girls at all. Don't they want to have sex too? It *is* enjoyable for them, right? Judging by what I've seen here in just the past two days, I have to go with a resounding yes.

Not that I told Cora she looked beautiful just as a way to get into her pants. My intentions were around ninety percent pure. I really thought she looked stunning in the water like that, so close to me.

And yet, clearly, so far away. The strand of her hair that came loose in the water is hanging down her back now, drying in the humid air, and I watch it bounce up and down as she walks with determination in front of me. Like she can't even stand to look into my eyes.

Maybe I've disgusted her. Which, honestly, upsets me. I like her too much for that.

But still. I can't help how I feel. They're called urges for a reason.

Maybe when I finally find Evan, I will swallow my pride and get him to teach me the ways of being a pussy magnet. Some nameless, faceless girl will help me get the deed done before I get drafted and sent to 'Nam and possibly die a virgin. I realize, with a start, that this hypothetical girl really is anonymous. I don't want to think of Amanda that way right now. Not after being in the water like that with Cora.

As we near the stage, there's a lull in the music and we hear someone making announcements. He asks for a doctor by name and then chastises some of the kids who are hanging off the scaffolding that surrounds the stage. Then he announces, "The warning that I've received, you might take it with however many grains of salt you wish, that the brown acid that is circulating around is not specifically too good. It is suggested that you stay away from that."

The warning brings back memories of this morning and—
in lieu of panic—a smile to my face.

Silently, I praise that brown acid to high heaven. What a
day I've already had, and I wouldn't have experienced any of
it without that tab. Specifically, not this girl's hand in mine,
which, despite the mixed signals, is what really matters here
and now. Well, that and meeting Janis.

Besides, I've finally decided that I am not going to die from
a bad trip. Not with a future doctor by my side.

chapter 43
Cora

The spot we find this time is on the hill that looks down onto the stage. After the announcements we just heard, I glance down at the scaffolding just below us and, sure enough, see people hanging off it. No doubt that's a medical emergency waiting to happen.

I still feel a little bit floaty from the pot, and slightly anxious to go back to feeling normal. I should've known better, really, since I like being in control of things, myself most of all. Taking a hit probably wasn't the brightest idea. I cross my arms tightly and squeeze my own sides, as if that will somehow contain my drifting thoughts.

There are a few cameras on cranes dotted close to the audience and one of them is blocking a large chunk of our view, which is already compromised by the darkening sky. Michael tells me that the band that's playing is called Mountain and he overheard that the Grateful Dead are coming on after. I like Mountain, I decide, and listen to the music eagerly despite the fact that I can't see them very well. Instead, I look around me as I listen, taking in the wild clothes (and, in some cases, rampant nudity) of my peers. Some distance away, up on the hill, I see some disturbed-looking cows, standing around in the grass. Just from their stance, I can tell they're bewildered. A small knot of people are eyeing them, and one approaches, kneeling down next to an udder.

"Oh, please, don't try to milk her," I mutter. It wouldn't end well for either of them.

After a few moments, I notice the person back away from the animal and I breathe a sigh of relief. Then I look around and really take in the destruction of Mr. Yasgur's dairy farm. Here and there, lone patches of grass resiliently hang on in seas of trampled brethren and mud. There are little piles of garbage peeking through like new sprouts, the shiny red of Coca-Cola cans in wild contrast to the green grass that should be there. Back near our lake, I see a dude with his back to me in a telltale pose. He is peeing.

It looks like a war zone.

And then I immediately feel guilty for thinking that because I suddenly remember Mark, who is in a real war zone.

I start to compose a letter to him in my head.

Dear Mark,

The greatest concert in the world has come to our little town. Can you believe it? A few hours ago, I sat five inches away from Janis Joplin. Actually, scratch that. We had a conversation.

Now, I'm about to hear the Grateful Dead and the Who.

I met a boy. . . .

I look over at Michael, who is resolutely turned to the stage, despite the fact that night has fallen and it's hard to discern much of anything down there. But the music plays on, the stars in the sky mirrored by the glowing tips of cigarettes and joints on the ground.

I take in his moonlit profile and wonder where this could possibly go. In a couple of days, he'll be back on his way to Massachusetts.

Eventually, Michael feels my stare and turns to me. "Good view?" he cracks.

I smile at him. Actually, it is. We've both been acting weird since we left the lake, lost in our own thoughts. Just like that, I close the gap and take his hand. And why shouldn't I? It's a moment and I have to seize it, just like all the kids around me living out their lives without fear. No fear of cops, of parents, of judgment. What makes me so different?

We stay like that as Mountain stops and the bands change.

"The Grateful Dead are fantastic," Michael says. "I think you'll really dig them."

I know a little about them, but not much, and Michael starts to explain how they are headquartered in San Francisco, sort of the mastheads of the whole hippie movement that really started there.

Before they take the stage, another announcement is made, this time advising anyone who is taking the green acid to get an airlift to the hospital.

"I think maybe I'll just stay away from acid while I'm here," Michael says.

"Good idea," I say.

"Though . . . would I still have my own personal doctor by my side if I did?" his eyes narrow mischievously.

"Candy striper," I say resolutely.

"Future doctor," Michael counters just as firmly and I feel such a huge surge of affection for him at that moment that I reach over and almost kiss him.

"Michael!" We are both startled by the yell and turn around in unison, our noses almost bumping against one another because of how close our faces are.

A group of five people is walking toward us, and it's only when I see the beautiful black one that I recognize them. They're Michael's friends, the ones from the tent yesterday. (Was that really yesterday? It seems like years ago.)

Immediately, I feel my hand being dropped, and I turn around to find Michael's face etched with worry.

I'm turned away from her, so I don't see the blonde as she comes barreling through, pushing me aside with an elbow before running into Michael's arms.

"There you are," she says, her voice muffled by his shoulder. "We've been looking everywhere for you!"

chapter 44
Michael

I hold on to Amanda tighter and longer than I should because I'm deathly afraid of what's going to happen once I let go and we have to talk. Counterproductive, I know. Especially because once we finally pull apart, she gives me one of her genuine, dazzling smiles, clearly pleased with the embrace.

I can't look Cora in the eye, so I observe the girl in front of me instead. She looks grimier than me; mud is streaked through her golden hair and on her clothes and body. A quick glance at the rest of my friends, and I can see they are in similar shape. Clearly, they didn't go for a dip in the lake like we did.

At the thought of the lake, I can't help but finally seek out Cora's face. Her expression is impossible to read, but she stands as if carved from stone.

"We were so worried about you," Amanda says. "We missed

you." I look back at her a moment too late, not before she has quickly followed my gaze to Cora. The smile disappears instantly.

"Who's she?" she asks sharply.

"Hey, it's the nurse, right?" Rob says as he walks over to Cora.

"Oh, right!" Evan joins in. "Thanks for taking care of him," he says as he slaps a friendly hand on Cora's shoulder.

Cora plasters on a smile and turns to them. "You're welcome."

"Where have you guys been?" Evan asks, and I feel Amanda's grip on me get tighter, echoing the question with her fingernails.

"Here," I say simply. "I've been looking for you guys too," I lie.

"Miss A even left you a note on a paper plate by the food stands," Evan says.

"Did you see it?" Catherine asks me, tilting her head. I can't tell if she actually looks at me suspiciously or if that's just my own projection.

I shake my head no. "I wish I had," I lie again and the words feel like tumbleweeds in my mouth. What am I saying? I refuse to look at Cora.

"It's okay," Amanda says. "We found you now."

I nod.

"Have you been eating?" she asks. "Did you get a sandwich from the helicopters?"

I nod again. "You?"

"Yes, we finally managed to get some. The food tents got an egg delivery this morning too and they made us omelets. I'm still pretty hungry but I'm holding out okay." She makes a brave face at the same time that I realize those omelets were likely from Cora's henhouse. "It's just incredible here, isn't it?"

"Yes," I finally say, unable to deny the truthfulness of that statement. It is incredible, or at least it was. I turn my head slightly so that I can spy Cora out of the corner of my eye. For whatever reason, I assumed she'd be looking over at us, trying to process my conversation with Amanda. But she's not. She's talking to Evan and Rob, her back turned to me almost entirely.

"Did you hear Joan Baez? She's been my favorite so far." I turn my attention back to the girl who is still in my arms, chattering away excitedly. I swallow something hard, a shard of truth probably, and I push it deep down. I don't want to examine it right now. In fact, I think I'm going to have to raid Evan's rucksack soon so that I'm in no state to feel much of anything. Not that I want to think too hard about Evan right now either, especially since I think I hear Cora laugh at something he just said.

I nod at everything Amanda says and eventually start talking too about the one thing I have a lot to say about: the music.

chapter 45
Cora

"Have you been enjoying the concert?" Rob asks me with a lovely smile on his face. Seriously, his teeth are whiter than Chiclet gum. I must ask him about his toothpaste.

Actually, forget toothpaste. I must smile and flirt like a pro here. I must avoid the blonde who is making my heart do strange things, like drop into my intestinal area. There's no reason for my heart to be anywhere other than my chest cavity. I should know; I have a very well-thumbed anatomy book.

"Very much," I say. "You?" Safe enough.

"Definitely. Santana was tremendous."

"Yes, he was cool," I reply genuinely. For once, I know exactly who he's talking about, thanks to Michael. There's a strange echo near my ribs again. I feel like slapping myself in the face and yelling "Snap out of it!" like I'm in the middle of an episode of *Days of Our Lives*.

From up on stage, the lead singer of the Grateful Dead is saying something about the green acid, lamenting how it's nowhere near as good as the stuff they have back home.

"You haven't had any bad trips or anything, have you?" I ask Rob.

"To be honest, I've been staying away after what happened to Michael. I don't think I'm ready to be a time god." He laughs.

"Wise," I say, and smile back at him.

From the corner of my eye, I think I can see Michael looking at us. I even think he's frowning. I subtly move closer to Rob and lightly touch his arm. I can feel his bicep even through the very tip of my fingers. He definitely should be a god of something; he's built like one.

"Are you looking forward to anyone else?" I ask.

"Oh, man. Everybody. Sly and the Family Stone. Jefferson Airplane. The Who. Janis. She's a down chick, right?"

"Yes!" I exclaim, and almost go on to tell him the story of how we just met Janis. But then I stop myself. How much of that story can I really tell? Are any of these people supposed to know I spent the whole day with Michael? Not that it's my job to cover for him, but still. Even though I can tell I'm operating on a whirlpool of emotions right now, including—very much—anger . . . it doesn't seem quite right to betray him.

The Grateful Dead are playing now, and we all just listen. At one point, there's a loud thump coming from one of the pieces of equipment, which sounds weird but I don't know enough about the music to discern whether it's not supposed to do that.

After about twenty minutes of music, Rob turns to me and Evan. "Not for nothing," he says. "But they sound pretty awful, man."

"No way, man," Evan protests. "Don't say that about the Dead."

"I'm not saying they usually sound awful. But today, something seems wrong," Rob says. He looks to me for support, but I shrug helplessly.

"They're amazing," Evan retaliates.

"Evan," Rob says. "Are you listening with your bong again?"

"Dude," Evan says. "I am almost totally straight. I haven't had anything in, like, forty-five minutes. You're the one tripping out."

"Boys, boys," I say. "Peace and music, right?"

"Of course, baby," Rob says. "Peace all the way. Even when your good friend has sadly lost his sense of hearing in a tragic mesc overdose."

Evan doesn't let that one go either, and I listen to some more of their good-natured banter. Eventually, the two other girls who were with them come closer to us and one, the shorter, darker one, puts a protective arm around Evan. It gives me a pang to realize that she's not entirely off base to look at me as if I'm a man-stealer. Wow. How did I let that happen exactly?

My increasing embarrassment is as good a reminder as any

to look at my watch and see how much time I have left before I need to mosey on home.

Er . . . four thirty? That can't be right. Either p.m. or, God forbid, a.m.

And then I remember that even though I took most everything else off, I forgot to take the watch off during my swim in the lake. Great. Waterlogged and completely useless.

I look around, trying to see a telltale gleam around anyone's wrist. There's only one in my vicinity. It's Amanda's.

Squashing down my guilt at being practically naked in her boyfriend's arms just a few hours ago, I get recklessly bold.

I step a bit closer to her and slap on a smile. "Hey, would you mind giving me the time?"

She looks startled that I'm talking to her and then her eyes narrow. I can almost see the wheels turning, figuring out a way to tell me to go to hell.

But really, how many snide remarks can you make to someone asking you the time?

So she settles for gritting her teeth and lifting up her left wrist like it's a Herculean task.

"Eleven twenty," she finally grunts.

"Holy shit!" I immediately exclaim, and I hear Michael laugh. Amanda and I turn to him with dual glares.

"It's not funny. I'm going to be murdered by my father." The smile immediately slides off his face. "I have to go."

I can see Michael almost start toward me, but then he stops, tethered to his spot by Amanda's hand.

I really have to go, and I have no idea what to say to him.

So I settle for a general "Nice to see you guys again" and a wave, which I mostly direct over to Rob, Evan, and the two girls instead of Michael.

Then I turn around and walk away at a quick trot.

I hear Michael call out, "Wait . . ." but then Amanda's voice cuts in.

"Wait for what?" she demands and then, luckily, I'm too far away to hear the rest.

I don't know whether to focus on the confusion I've just left behind or the certain doomsday that's ahead of me.

Neither will help my state of mind, I finally decide. But there's nothing to do but keep walking, so I time my steps to the beat of the music for as long as I can hear it.

chapter 46
Michael

I can't even watch Cora walk away. Amanda is asking me why I called out for her and I don't have a proper answer at all, but I know I can't continue to stare after her.

So I do something horrific.

I kiss Amanda to shut her up. It feels awful. I don't mean the kiss itself or Amanda. I mean me. Knots of guilt are forming in my throat, making it hard to breathe (especially while kissing, where breathing is already a carefully choreographed sport). I kiss Amanda and I think about Cora and wish she were the one here with me now.

Which, of course, makes me a really shitty person.

All this time, I've assumed that Amanda would eventually cheat on me. In fact, just a couple of days ago, wasn't I hoping for it? With Rob? But she didn't. It was me. Maybe she's been right to be preemptively pissed at me this whole time. Maybe

I am a loser and she is, after all, way out of my league.

I've been feeling so much inner turmoil that the Grateful Dead have switched over to Creedence and I've hardly noticed. I don't think I could even tell you one thing about the Dead's set.

Now Creedence is playing "Bad Moon Rising," a faster-paced version than they normally play, and the word "bad" cuts through the humid night air, headed straight for me. *I've been a bad boyfriend*, I think as I look at the top of Amanda's head. She seems calmer now, swaying to the music. She looks like she should be on the cover of a magazine, like the poster child for our generation or something. A little mud-speckled, a flower still drawn on her cheek, long blond hair, blue eyes. Woodstock's dream girl.

But not for me. For me, it was a striped apron and someone who couldn't even tell Hendrix from Townshend. Someone who didn't come for the music at all, who came just to help. Someone who helped *me* by making everything seem in focus for once. After all the time I've spent with Evan relishing things going fuzzy, it's funny that it's the exact opposite that has made me feel the lightest I've ever been.

But she's gone now. And what can I do about it? I can't run away from my friends again and show up at her doorstep. Her dad definitely seems like the type who owns a shotgun and knows how to use it. I can't even break up with Amanda. Not for a . . . whatever . . . that would last one more day at the very most. And that is only if Cora ever talks to me again. Or, for that matter, if I ever even see her again.

I can't do anything.

Can I?

Creedence starts a new song, and after a few moments I recognize it. It's a cover of a song my mom owns actually, one of her beloved jazz records. Nina Simone, I think. "I Put a Spell on You."

Black magic really must be at work because soon I'm thinking, *Maybe I'll see Cora at her medical tent tomorrow*. Even though I shouldn't think that at all. What would be the point of seeing her when I have Amanda and home and a whole life nowhere near Bethel, New York, starting the day after tomorrow?

But it doesn't matter. Hope doesn't listen to logic. And by the end of the song, I'm pretty sure it's not hope at all. I will see Cora tomorrow because I will make it happen. What do they call that?

Oh. I think it's determination.

All in all, a totally foreign feeling for me.

Sunday, August 17

chapter 47
Cora

It's past midnight by the time I arrive home. I guess I stopped walking briskly as soon as I was out of Michael's sight, feeling heavy and sluggish because of everything I was walking from and walking to. What difference does twenty minutes here or there make anyway? I'm dead meat no matter what. Dead meat with the stench of someone else's boyfriend on her lips. In an instant, this day has gone from exhilarating to disastrous.

Approaching my house, I'm surprised to see that all the lights are off. I was sure the house would be blazing, that there'd be neighbors strewn across our front yard organizing themselves for the search, and that Mom would have resurrected the nuclear raid siren. Instead, everything is still and silent and nothing but crickets greet me at my door.

I try to let myself in and am surprised when the front

doorknob meets me with resistance. Locked. We never lock our doors here, and I immediately can't help but wonder whether it's punishment against me or a precaution against the hordes of hippies my father thinks might come barreling through.

It takes me a moment to remember there is a spare key under the doormat. It's covered in dust and cobwebs when I find it, but I fish it out and unlock the door.

I tiptoe in, still amazed at the silence. Out of curiosity, I head into the kitchen and glance at the cuckoo clock on the wall, just in case Amanda played a trick on me with the time and it's really ten o'clock. But nope, it's after midnight.

I turn around to go up to my room, and am greeted by a solid wall of shadow. "Cora." It spits out my name. I jump a mile.

The lights get switched on and the shadow becomes a fuming, squat man glaring at me. Dad.

"What," he says in a dangerously quiet voice, "is the meaning of this?"

"Dad," I say, my heart pounding from the scare and from the dread of what's about to happen. "I'm sorry. Time just ran away from me. . . ."

He shakes his head. "Time *ran away* from you? What happened to your watch?"

Dad points at my wrist and I quickly draw my hand away. I don't think telling him my watch died because I was skinny-dipping in the lake with a boy is going to help defuse the situation.

"It's just been so busy," I start to quickly say. "And then the music was so good, I just lost track. . . ."

"That. Goddamn. Music," he seethes. "Do you really think you can use that horrible, drugged-out assault on humanity as an excuse? For coming home *after midnight?*"

I grimace. "No, sir," I say. Probably best to just get this over with.

"For the rest of this weekend, you will stay right in this house."

My eyes widen. "But . . ."

"You will help out your mother and me around the farm. You won't leave our sight for the next forty-eight hours."

"Dad . . . ," I begin.

"And then maybe in a few weeks we can discuss whether you can even go back to the hospital again."

I stare at him. "You can't ban me from the hospital."

"I most certainly can."

"For coming home an hour after curfew?" I say incredulously.

"Because Bethel is declared a war zone and you're in the trenches, *enjoying the music*, as you say."

My heart rate is still up, but this time I can feel the anger that's surging through my blood. "This isn't a war zone, Dad," I start out calmly enough. "Mark is in a war zone." But then I can't stop myself. "And do you know who are the only people trying to get him out? Those damn hippies you're always going on about."

"Get him out?" he counters. "By doing what? Carrying

signs and getting high? Those spoiled kids who have no idea what a real battlefield is like? Or what an honor it is to fight in one?"

"I'm pretty sure Mark doesn't think it's an honor. Not anymore," I mutter.

He snorts. "And just what would you know about it? Your brother is out there fighting for . . ."

"For what exactly? I'd love to know. Give me one good reason Mark is being shot at instead of being here with us."

"For his country," Dad says with finality. As if that should answer everything.

Now it's my turn to snort. "What does a government halfway across the world have to do with our country?"

"For freedom. Those people . . ."

"Want him out of their country, I'm assuming," I say in a mocking tone.

Which might be the final straw for my father. "You don't know anything, girl," he shouts, his dangerous whisper now blossomed into full-volume wrath. "And you should learn to shut up about things you know nothing about."

Here's the thing with me. My dad gets visibly angry often, but I don't. But when I do, you can take seven times his anger and still not be able to fill up the hot-air balloon of rage that inflates inside me, just waiting to be untethered.

"NO," I yell back. "I will not shut up. And I know plenty, Dad." I say "Dad" all drawn out, like it's a joke to call him that. "I know about medicine and surgery and educated people. I know more than some hick farmer from fucking Anytown, USA, *ever* will."

I stay just long enough to see his eyes widen. Then, without thinking, I push past him, and run right out the front door.

chapter 48
Michael

Janis is onstage now, and she's killing it. It's so dark that I can hardly make her out at all; she's just a silhouette with big floating sleeves. But I can hear every word that she sings, every note drawn out with passion and conviction. It's hard to believe this is the same soft-spoken person we came across at a hotel bar just earlier today.

It's hard to believe at all. Where I was today. Who I was with.

I can't believe Cora's not here with me to hear Janis. Not after Janis called her "sister."

A brass section wails on Janis's song and I watch the top of Amanda's head in front of me, moving in time to the music. In the dark of night, I can almost pretend her hair is jet black, that she is someone else entirely.

And that's completely unfair, isn't it? If there's one thing

Janis's voice is pleading with me to do, it's this: Man up. I should tell Amanda that it's over.

And then, as if I dreamt her back into life, Cora is suddenly beside us again. I stare at her, for a moment positive it's a hallucination, even though I haven't taken anything all day. But then I see Rob grin at her too.

"Hey, Miss Cora is back," he says.

Everyone turns to her now and she gives a wave and a smile back, but it's directed at Rob. She hardly even looks at me. "Figured I can't really miss the greatest rock concert of all time when it's right in my backyard. Right?"

"No, ma'am," Rob counters.

She walks over to him and I follow her with my eyes. Trying to think of something to say. Amanda looks from my face to Cora's, a scowl screwing up her features.

"What about your dad murdering you?" Amanda demands of Cora.

"Yeah," Cora says. "Screw him."

My jaw almost drops. Cora is a surprising girl but I still never expected her to say that.

Rob laughs, though. "Yeah, screw all the parents," he says.

Cora smiles. "Screw all the parents!"

Rob takes the opportunity to lift her hand and then spin her around underneath it before bringing his arms behind her back to end in an impressive dip. Cora laughs.

Smooth freakin' asshole.

"This is Janis, right?" Cora asks him.

"The one and only," he responds.

"Do you know I met her today?"

"What? Get out of here, you big liar," Rob says.

"Nuh-uh," she says. "Totally met her." And I immediately realize she said "*I* met her," not "*we* met her."

She launches into a version of our story that doesn't include me and I feel like shit.

Cora is here, but she's really not. She's not here with me.

chapter 49
Cora

After I tell Rob my story, I listen to Janis Joplin, really listen to her, for the first time. I've heard a song or two from her before but before today, she wasn't a real person to me. She wasn't someone you could have a conversation with, someone who could buy you a drink.

Now that she is, I think I finally understand why someone would be so obsessed with music. Everything Janis is and has ever felt, she's pouring out onto the stage right now. She's inviting us all in to witness it. It takes my breath away, the bravery of it.

Eventually—too soon—Janis's set ends and Rob gets extra-excited because Sly and the Family Stone come on next. I can't make out much on the stage; the lights they have up there don't seem powerful enough to counter the darkness of a country night. But I can tell there are a lot of band members and, of course, as soon as the music starts the vibe completely changes. This is dancing, party music and all around me, people are jumping around and swaying wildly.

Rob takes me for another spin and I let him. Every time I twirl or swing or dip I keep my eyes trained to look away from Michael. It's pretty impressive, actually. Like my own psychological choreography.

About a half hour into their set, Sly asks the audience to join him in a sing-along. "Most of us need approval from our neighbors," he starts out, before asking us to shun that concept and sing the word "higher" with him, throwing our peace signs into the air. "It'll do you no harm," he claims.

At first, I just watch everyone around me following suit. But then Rob grabs my hand and makes me pump it into the air. "Get into it!" he yells, as he starts yelling "higher" in time with the rest of the crowd.

I smile and say it softly at first, but as it goes on and on and everyone is shouting, I do too. Why shouldn't I? "Still again, some people feel that they shouldn't," Sly says from the stage, again encouraging us to "get in on something that could do you some good" without worry about embarrassment or approval. I realize Sly is speaking directly to me. I raise my arm higher, wave my two fingers in the air, and yell into the damp night. The red Hog Farm fabric still wrapped around my wrist glows bright against the starry sky like a triumphant banner. I close my eyes to savor how amazing it all feels.

Except that emblazoned on the back of my eyelids is the silhouette of a person I haven't looked at in hours. Michael.

I immediately open my eyes and fix them on Rob, whose head is swinging wildly to the music.

Rob is beautiful, just like when I first saw him. He's also energetic, fun, and funny. Most importantly, he doesn't do weird things to my stomach or make me think too hard about things like feelings. Feelings are crap. That's why I'm going to be a doctor, dealing with the wonderful, solid world of physical ailments.

Sly has gone into the "higher" chorus again and it's louder than ever, now that everyone is taking his advice and not waiting for approval from their neighbors.

I don't need approval either, I finally realize. I will be a doctor, no matter what anyone thinks or says.

I say "higher" one extra time than everyone else, not realizing the song has ended and they've already broken into applause. But I don't care. I'm sure I clap harder than anyone else too. Something has just become so very clear to me about myself, about who I am, and I have the music to thank for it.

Which, I guess, is what Michael was trying to tell me just this afternoon.

chapter 50
Michael

I glimpse the time on Amanda's watch. It's past five a.m. when the real Roger Daltrey saunters onto the stage.

As the night has gone on, some space has cleared up (I guess some people actually want to get sleep or something, the idiots) and we've all managed to get pretty close to the stage now, so I can see Roger clearly in all his glory. He looks like a scarecrow with a mop of wild blond hair. He's wearing an open jacket with long, fringed white sleeves, and no shirt underneath, his taut belly on display. The band starts to play and he actually prowls onstage, walking it from one end to the other like he owns every fucking audience member.

And you know what? I think he does. He sings and gyrates, exuding some crazy confidence and something else. Let's call it raw manliness. I can practically hear the sighs from all the female, and probably some male, concertgoers around me. I think Amanda is turning to putty beside me. And I'm sure everyone else not completely beguiled by him just wants to be him.

I know I do.

I can't help it. I turn my head slightly and seek out Cora's face. She's been completely wrapped up in Rob this whole time, ignoring me at every turn. But she must feel me looking at her and, this time, she meets my gaze. She looks up at the specimen of testosterone on the stage. And then she looks back at me again. Then she laughs quietly.

I should feel hurt or like my own manhood is being mocked. But the truth is, she's right. I ain't no Roger Daltrey. And the fact that anyone would ever mistake me for him is pretty hilarious. So I start chuckling too.

I decide to risk it further. "You think the suit dropped some brown acid too?" I yell over to her, referring, of course, to the executive who mistook me for Roger.

Cora glances at the stage one more time before turning her gaze back to me. She just smiles enigmatically and I smile back.

But then she returns her gaze to the stage again and she doesn't look toward me anymore, even though I keep waiting for her to. I think I've lost my moment. And her.

Eventually, I give up and focus on the band again. I see Keith Moon freaking out behind the drums, probably tripping out on something. Or maybe just the music itself. It is that good. I see Pete Townshend with his guitar, his dark, close-cropped hair and long face in direct contrast to Roger's bright demeanor. Pete is in all white. When he plays, he plays angry, like he's seeking revenge from the strings.

Between them—and let's not forget the fantastic bassist, John Entwistle—there is so much palpable energy radiating from that stage. At five in the fucking morning.

It's beautiful. And for a moment I let myself realize that being a fake part of that for even just a minute in some stuffy corporate dude's eyes is absolutely priceless.

I bang my head just a little bit harder and move around just a little bit more as they play. At one point I begin to realize I'm mimicking Roger's moves a little. But you know what? I don't care. I had rock star confidence for an hour today. And if I can somehow get that back, I'm pretty sure I can rule the world.

chapter 51
Cora

Ten songs in and Roger Daltrey continues to slither around onstage like some sort of sexy snake. I've never had much of a rock star complex—at least not before Michael's earth-shattering kiss today—but this guy makes it hard not to feel just a little bit flustered. And you know what, I have to admit that Michael *does* resemble him. They're both long and lean, with a similar mess of blond, wavy, shoulder-length hair; I don't think the suit was that far off.

Seeing Mr. Daltrey now, I can't help but smile at the perfectly magical, one-of-a-kind experience Michael and I shared thanks to him. I break my eye-contact rule with Michael just long enough to try to convey that.

The band is in between songs when a man with dark curly hair climbs up on the stage. I vaguely recognize him. I think he might have been one of the extra guys who was helping out in the medical tent this morning.

He grabs the mic that Pete Townshend (Rob reminded me of his name) was using while the guitarist is turned away fiddling with an amp. "I think this is a pile of shit while John Sinclair rots in prison."

There is some confusion in the air, but I also hear the crowd applauding, Rob included. Because of Wes, I vaguely know who Sinclair is—a political activist who was recently sentenced to ten years in jail for selling a couple of joints to undercover cops.

But now Pete Townshend has turned around. He brings his guitar up like an ax and the mic picks up most of his words. "Fuck off my fucking stage!" he yells, and brings the guitar down on the curly-haired man, who either falls or leaps off the stage. I strain my neck and look for him, to make sure he's not on the ground, injured, but he's disappeared into the crowd.

Something heavy and almost silent hangs in the air now. We just witnessed a moment of violence in what has, until now, been a dreamy couple of days of peace and music—just like the posters promised. It's a jarring reminder of the world outside our bubble. The world of war and racism and assassinations. I can tell I'm not the only one who suddenly remembers how thin that bubble's skin is.

In my disturbed mood, I think about my father. I can't believe I cursed in front of him. Or called him a dumb hick.

I'm not sure I'll ever forget the look in his eyes when I stormed out, like I ripped his heart and his voice box out at the same time. Speechless through and through.

I may not always agree with him, and sometimes he makes it so easy to disregard him with his outdated views. He trusts the US government completely, but not young people. He gets behind the word "democracy," but not Wes's passion for carrying his sign. It's like he wants so badly for the world to be black and white when it's not. It's not even shades of gray. It's every color in the world: all the beautiful ones, the grotesque ones, and everything in between.

I have to remind myself that my dad hasn't had it easy. His own mother refused to talk to him after he married Mom. And then she died within a year. And even though I can see his chest puff up every time he brings up his wars, I've never really asked him about what that experience was actually like. He did get shot, for God's sake.

And I know he loves us. I knew it when I was five and he saved my favorite pig from slaughter even though he had told me time and again not to get attached. I knew it when he made sure to buy Wes not just the toy soldiers but the exact ones he asked for, even though he had to drive to another town fifty miles away. And then when he taught all three of us how to drive with an astounding amount of patience, especially in light of Mark's propensity for hitting our mailbox every other time he parked.

Today, when he came at me, he expected it to be like all his other histrionics and, surely, he thought he was in the right since I had blatantly broken the rules. He never expected me to talk back. Never expected me to say *that*.

I feel ashamed.

Now the Who are playing "My Generation" and all my dark, murky thoughts are further mucked up by Ned. I wonder if he's here to hear his favorite song, and suddenly I feel completely exhausted. The ping-pong of today's emotions has been almost too much to bear.

So when the Who play one more song and then bid us good night, I know it's time for me to go as well. I need to sleep. Maybe, as my mom is always fond of saying, everything will look better in the morning. Maybe my dad will get a miraculous bout of short-term amnesia.

"I have to go," I tell Rob. "I'm so sleepy."

"Just stay and sleep here," he responds. "We have bags."

I shake my head no. "I can't. I have to go back to work tomorrow." As long as I'm not chained to my room when I wake up. "They need me in the medical tent." Except they don't really. Nobody needs a seventeen-year-old candy striper.

God. Apparently the self-pity comes on strong when I'm beat.

But truly, I have to go.

"Good-bye," I say, and this time I look directly in Michael's face when I say it. I'm preparing myself to never see him again.

Still, we had one really excellent day together. So I can

afford to give him a smile before I get swept up by Rob, who gives me a sloppy kiss on the cheek.

"Thanks," I say, before I turn around and leave, not even looking back to examine the jealousy likely scrawled on Michael's face. That's not how I want to remember him.

chapter 52
Michael

After the Who's epic twenty-five-song set, we all realize we need to get some sleep. It seems like they're breaking down equipment anyway, so I'm not too upset when the girls suggest we find a place to hunker down for the night.

We walk away from the stage until we find an unoccupied bit of land near the top of the big hill. I have my backpack again, and the sleeping bag along with it. Amanda crawls into it with me with barely a word and passes out right away.

But I can't sleep. Not too long ago, Cora said good-bye to me like it was for real, like it was the last time we'd ever see each other. But I won't believe that to be true. Not in a place as magical and epic as Woodstock.

Suddenly the sleeping bag and the girl crammed into it with me are stifling and I know I have to get out of it. As quietly as I can, I pull the zipper, move Amanda's arm off me, and roll out. She shifts a little but doesn't wake up.

For good measure, I move a little farther away before I lie back down on the grass. It feels better out in the open, but still not quite right. I look up at the stars that seemed to hold so much meaning for me just a couple of nights ago. They're inscrutable now, nothing but balls of gas burning billions of miles away. They tell me nothing about what I should do or who I should be.

My eyelids feel heavy and I know I'm drifting in and out of sleep because the sky seems to be getting lighter each time I open my eyes. At some point, I hear a faraway voice announcing, "This is morning maniac music!"

And then the music starts up again. It doesn't take me long to recognize Grace Slick's distinctive growl.

I close my eyes and try to feel everything. The slick, dewy grass beneath my back. The morning breeze that tickles the little hairs in my nose. The distinctive smell of mud and skin. And, of course, the sound of Jefferson Airplane rocking out just down the hill from me.

The only thing I know for sure is that it's technically the last day of the festival. I need to make it count.

chapter 53
Cora

The house is quiet and dark when I approach it again. I'm not terribly surprised. I honestly don't expect to see my dad around now, not after what I said and my storming out.

It's almost six a.m. and I'm pretty tired. Still, I decide to hop into the shower before I grab a couple of hours of sleep. The lake can't really count as bathing, can it? I try not to think about that time in the water too much as I quickly lather up and rinse off. I try not to remember Michael's face or the way his eyes sparkled with reflected water and desire for me. I try not to feel the ghost of his hands around my waist.

I say I try. I don't say I succeed.

I set my alarm for ten a.m. and go to sleep with my hair wet. I don't sleep well. The damp pillow doesn't help and neither do all the day's events running through my mind.

Both the sublime (riding in a helicopter with Michael) and the shameful (yelling at my dad) parts of it.

Still, I'm dead asleep when the alarm finally buzzes, and I get out of bed red-eyed and groggy. My hair has curled messily and there's nothing to do but braid it. I dress quickly, slipping into one of my comfortable floral summer dresses, leaving the red flying pig bandanna hanging from my chair. I don't have time to think about looking hip today.

I'm glad I took a shower last night so that I won't have to take one this morning. My plan is to make it from my room to the front door in one shot and see if I can get out without seeing my dad. I'd like to get to the festival without a scene. By ten thirty in the morning, he should be out on the farm already, three hours after breakfast and two away from lunch. With any luck, my mom won't be in the kitchen either. I'm not sure what he told her last night, but I'm in no mood to find out. I will deal with it all later. When the festival has left and I am prepared to face the consequences. I can't miss this last day of being in the middle of the only thing the country's talking about. It'll probably never happen to me again.

My luck holds out and I make it out of the house without seeing anyone. I haven't eaten anything, but it doesn't matter. As I told Michael, we can survive without food for a long time, and I now know where to get water. I wonder if the army's going to drop off sandwiches again too.

I make it to my medical tent at around five to eleven. From a few feet outside it, I hear some screaming and quicken my pace.

I walk in and search for the distressed patient. She's easy to find. She's in a corner with Anna and she's in labor.

Anna quickly looks over at me and says, "Could you get some towels?" by way of greeting. I do so right away, happy to be busy.

When I walk over to the patient, I suddenly recognize her and the bearded man sitting with her. They were the couple with the oranges on Friday. I smile at them warmly, remembering their kindness. Despite her pain, the mother-to-be smiles back at me.

For the next hour, I spend a lot of time trying to soothe her with cool towels, tea, and—more often—by allowing her to squeeze my hand as tightly as she wants. I can tell by her husband's face across her stomach that both of our fingers might be useless after today.

One of the doctors in the tent keeps glancing nervously at me. I don't recognize him—he must be from another hospital—but I hear him ask Anna if she's sure it's a good idea to have "the girl" dealing with the pregnant woman.

"I think you'll find us girls know a lot on the subject," Anna says to him coldly. "Now, I think there are some bloodied feet you can tend to in that corner over there. Doctor." I smile into my hair.

Twenty minutes later, Anna comes over and takes a peek at my patient's dilation status.

"Okay." She nods to the mother. "There's a helicopter here to take you to the hospital and I think you're good to get on it."

"We can't have the baby here?" the husband asks.

"It's going to be safer at the hospital," Anna says as they help the mother up.

I walk out with them and watch them get on the helicopter, all the time trying not to think too hard about helicopters. Or oranges. I find I'm swallowing a lot.

After they've safely taken off, Anna walks back to the tent with me. "How was your day yesterday?" she asks.

"It was fine," I say.

"Did you have fun?" she asks.

"Yes. It was great," I say. And then, thankfully, we are hit with another influx of patients, and neither of us has any time for more questions.

chapter 54
Michael

I drift in and out as Jefferson Airplane plays on, and by the time I fully wake up, there's no music at all. I walk over to look at Amanda's watch. It's noon.

The sky is overcast and cloudy. It looks like it's going to rain again.

"I feel so disgusting," Amanda says as she gets up and looks down at her muddy arms. Then she looks over at my clothes, which are still caked with the stuff from yesterday and again today, and looks even more bewildered. "So are you," she says matter-of-factly.

I guess now that I have my backpack, I can switch into the change of clothing I brought. I slowly bring the bag over and swap my shirt for the Monterey Pop T-shirt that's balled up at the bottom.

For a second, I think about suggesting the lake to Amanda,

but then I decide against it. I don't want to taint that memory. I want it to stay as perfect and pristine as it is.

It doesn't matter because Evan suggests it anyway. So after rolling up our sleeping bags and gathering our meager belongings, we head on over to the water.

The lake is even more crowded than it was yesterday because I guess even some of the holdouts can't spend three muddy days without a bath.

Amanda, Catherine, Suzie, Evan, and Rob all strip down to their birthday suits and wade in. I linger back.

When she's only in up to her thighs, Amanda turns around and yells at me to come join them.

I'm still fully clothed and I don't want to. I look at her stunning naked body and feel sick to my stomach. Her skin is porcelain pale, glowing in the weak sun. I have been begging her to let me see her like this for months. And now I just want to turn away.

But what excuse can I give her? Slowly, I strip down completely too and leave my clothes in a pile next to the others'. When I get in the lake, I stay closer to Evan and Suzie than I do Amanda. I don't want to touch her in that water. It became sacred to me yesterday and I'm already ruining that.

I can see Amanda's thinking about swimming over, though, so I dunk myself in, rub my arms a little bit, and then start to wade back out again.

"Hey . . . ," Amanda calls.

"I'm worried about our clothes," I lie. "I'll go stand guard."

I change quickly, putting on the clean jeans I brought and

the Monterey shirt. Then I wait, purposely not looking out at my friends but keeping my eyes on the horizon.

Eventually, they splash out too. Amanda takes her time rummaging through my backpack for the clean dress she brought, bending over so that her ass is a hairline away from me. I look away.

Everyone gets dressed and the music still hasn't started. Rob suggests we go to the food tents to see if we can get something to eat. It's only then that I think to ask him what happened to the girl he was supposed to be meeting here.

"She never made it, since the roads were already closed by the time she was supposed to leave," Rob says, and shrugs.

"Shame," I say, thinking mostly about his flirt session with Cora from the night before. But Rob just shrugs again and grins.

The food tents are handing out more army-issued bologna sandwiches. We each get one and Catherine suggests a picnic by the lake. We go to the drinkable side.

Our picnic ends and still no music, so Suzie brings up the woods that surround the farm. "I heard they're selling things in there."

"What sort of things?" Evan perks up and I'm sure he's thinking about getting more weed.

"T-shirts and stuff like that," Suzie says.

We have nothing better to do, so we go.

chapter 55
Cora

At around one, Ned shows up at the tent. He's volunteering today.

Turns out, he was volunteering yesterday, too. I know this because as soon as he comes in, he walks right up to me and says, "I thought you'd be here yesterday."

"What?" I respond, a little disoriented by the lack of greeting.

"I thought we'd both be here volunteering together yesterday."

"Oh," I say, as I brew up some more freak-out tea. You would think all the announcements about the acid would have stemmed some of the tide of bad trips, but you'd be wrong. Maybe it only freaked me and Michael out. Or maybe we were just looking for an easy excuse to spend time together. "Anna gave me the day off," I tell Ned. "To see the festival." I leave it at that.

"Oh, really? How was it?"

"Great," I say.

"Great," Ned says to me, and smiles. "I mean, obviously, I could hear some of the music from here. But it must have been cool to watch it, right?"

"Yeah," I say, and busy myself with pouring tea and delivering it to a couple sitting in the corner.

Ned gets some orders himself and starts to treat some minor wounds. But I notice that every time he needs something from somewhere else in the tent, he manages to find a way to walk by me and say something.

The first time it's "Who was your favorite person you saw yesterday?"

"Janis Joplin," I answer honestly, thinking not only of her spectacular performance but of meeting her at the hotel bar.

The next time he walks by, he's had time to think about this response and he asks me, "Was Janis Joplin on yesterday? I don't remember hearing her."

"Yeah," I say. "She was on really late."

"How late?"

"I think around two a.m."

He frowns, about to say something else, but I walk away to tend to a patient.

He finds a way to be where I am within five minutes. "Your dad let you stay out until two a.m.?" he asks incredulously.

"Not exactly," I say.

"You snuck out?" he asks, and he lightly touches my shoulder for no particular reason.

I look him in the eyes then, those brown eyes that used to make me feel so warm and happy, like holding a freshly baked cookie on your tongue. "Not exactly," I say mysteriously, and give him a small smile before I go to a young boy with a twisted ankle. The boy is slightly hysterical and therefore, thankfully, needs my full attention for a while. Ned isn't able to get to me, but at one point, I catch him looking thoughtfully in my direction. It's like he knows, like he can feel the sea change between us.

Anna, never missing anything, must see the quick glance Ned and I share. Next time she's near me, she voices my exact thought. "They always know," she says.

I look at her, both of us understanding exactly what she's talking about. "Do they?" I ask.

She nods. "When you're just about ready to move on, they know. And that's usually when they come back. It's like the universe's way of making you figure out what you really want."

She leaves me to cut up more bandages and I have a perfect view of the back of Ned's head as he tends to someone.

How will I pass this test? Am I ready to move on? Move on to what, though? A boy I might never see again? One who lives hundreds of miles way and who, not to mention, has a gorgeous girlfriend. Okay, a bitchy girlfriend, but gorgeous nonetheless.

I look at Ned's soft brown hair, see the one piece in the back that always seems to stick up. I watch the familiar shadow his body casts across the floor and know there was a time when I delighted in seeing that tall, assured shadow holding hands with mine—like the pavement itself was painted with our love.

And I know that something in my heart has changed. That little lump that was always embedded somewhere in my throat whenever I saw him; that little surge of adrenaline; even that ounce of fear of losing him that was always brimming just below the surface when we were together.

It's all gone.

Instead, unencumbered by butterflies in my stomach or a stuttering heartbeat, I finally imagine what staying with Ned really would have entailed. If we'd gotten married someday, he would be doing what he always did: making decisions for both of us. For our entire family. And who would I be? A wife and mother, I presume. But not a doctor.

In other words, I wouldn't be me at all.

Throughout all my pining and heartbreak, how did I miss this one kernel of cold, hard truth that would have made it much easier to get over him after all?

chapter 56
Michael

I wish Cora and I had thought to come to these woods together. They are wild and fun. They are also the same woods that we were camping by on the first night. Evan recognizes the way to his pharmacy immediately.

Just as Suzie said, there are vendors spread out among the trees, a lot of them selling homemade tie-dyed T-shirts, some with hilariously rude sayings. One of the shirts has a doodle of the moon landing with the big words "GOVERNMENT HOAX" surrounding it. That guy works impressively fast, considering the landing was all of a few weeks ago.

"Nice shirt," the guy says to me when he sees me looking at his wares. I think he must be trying to hawk something from his table, but when I look up, he's actually pointing to the T-shirt I'm wearing. "Were you there?"

"I wish," I respond, wondering if I had more of an

enterprising spirit, could I really have made it out to California as a sixteen-year-old?

"I was there," the man reminisces.

"Which was better?" I have to ask. The Monterey Pop festival in '67 was legendary, but I'm really starting to think Woodstock might surpass its fame. Though, perhaps, that's wishful thinking on my part since this is the one I'm here for.

The guy grins. "It's *all* groovy," he says emphatically, and points behind me. I turn around to see three thin wooden signs tacked to a tree. Each one has an arrow pointing in a different direction and a label: GROOVY WAY, GENTLE PATH, HIGH WAY.

I turn back to the T-shirt guy with a smile. But he has a more serious expression on his face now when he gives me this unexpected bout of wisdom. "There's no wrong way. Wherever you're at, you have to make it what you want it to be."

I look back at him, really mulling over his words. "Thanks," I say as I walk away, and I mean it, looking at the painted words of the signs one more time as I pass them.

So anywhere I am can be the Groovy Way, or Gentle Path, or High Way? I suppose anywhere could be a billion other adjectives too. Is all of life really just a state of mind? I'm not even currently a time god, and all these thoughts are suddenly rushing my brain in a rare moment of waking clarity.

Everything is better at Woodstock.

The girls are crowded around a small jewelry stand, looking over beaded necklaces and peace-sign bracelets. As

I'm hanging back, letting them browse, a stone catches my eye.

I move forward to look more closely at it. It's a large glass stone, a murky blue with streaks of darker blue within it. It's shaped like a teardrop and hangs from a thin chain.

It instantly reminds me of being in the rain-pattered lake with Cora. The colors, the shape, everything about it. I want to buy it for her so badly.

I ask the price. "Ten dollars," the lady says to me.

I don't think I have ten dollars but, just in case, I check my backpack thoroughly. I ask the lady if she'd be willing to take four dollars and thirty-seven cents for it. She declines.

"Awww, it's beautiful," I hear Amanda say behind me, and I turn around to see her beaming at me. "But it's okay, babe. That's expensive."

I just nod, but don't say anything to correct her mistaken impression that the necklace would be for her. Because I am the scum of the earth, that's why.

I get the uncomfortable feeling that I'm not the only one who thinks that either. Looking up, I find the source of my paranoia. It's Cora's brother, standing at a nearby booth with his friends, his eyes boring into me, as if he were brought to life by the intensity of my thoughts. I wish my thoughts were good enough to bring his sister here instead. But then again, I don't know if I'd want the dirty look that Wes is giving me to ever cross Cora's face. Definitely not directed at me, anyway.

And that's when I realize: It's time for me to take the High Way. Even though the music is about to start soon and I don't want to miss it. Even though I'm terrified about the wrath I'm about to bring upon myself. None of that really matters. How can I instruct Cora to listen to the music and let it tell her to believe in herself, when I can't do the same thing? Everything the past few days have been telling me is that it's time to man up, to own something that I know is the right thing to do.

Evan has already made his purchases and the group is making its way back out of the woods. I hurry to catch up with them and lightly touch Amanda's arm. It's the first time I've voluntarily touched her all day.

She turns around, megawatt smile and all. She's probably still thinking about that necklace. I take a deep breath and watch as our friends keep going, not realizing that we've stopped. I ask her if we can talk.

"Course," she says.

"This is all me," I blurt. "All my fault." I figure I should start this off with one of her favorite phrases. Anyway, it's the truth.

"What is?" she asks suspiciously. "That you didn't have money for the necklace?"

"No, not that," I say firmly, and something about the way I say it makes her smile begin to falter. "I just . . . I don't know why you're with me, Amanda. I seem to piss you off all the time. And I think, I don't know. We should be happier than this."

"Happier?" she says slowly.

"Yes. You deserve more. . . ."

"Happier . . . ," she says again, in an oddly detached voice. "I don't think I understand, exactly. . . ." She tilts her head at me, blinking like a Disney doe.

I take her hand and then a deep breath, staring into her clear blue eyes. "Amanda . . . ," I begin.

But I don't get to finish my sentence. I get a tap on the shoulder, and when I instinctively turn around, I don't even have time to register what's happening before something explodes near my right eye and everything goes black.

chapter 57
Cora

From the tent, I hear Mr. Yasgur get introduced as the owner of the farm and then, after a smattering of applause, his gentle, slightly stilted voice comes through on the loudspeaker. I can practically picture him up there, with his dark curly hair and thick, square glasses, looking for sure like somebody's accountant.

"I think you people have proven something to the world. Not only to the town of Bethel, or Sullivan County, or New York State. You've proven something to the world. This is the largest group of people ever assembled in one place," Mr. Yasgur says, before going on to thank the producers of the festival and to acknowledge that the lack of food and water must have been a hardship.

"But above that," he continues, his voice echoing across his own fields, "the important thing that you've proven to the world is that half a million kids—and I call you kids because I have children that are older than you are—a half million young people can get together and have three days of fun and music and have nothing but fun and music and . . ." He seems to get a little choked up. "God bless you for it," he finishes.

I hear all the people he was just complimenting and blessing applaud for him loudly, with catcalls and whistles, just like he was one of the rock stars up on that stage. I can't help but smile. I admire Mr. Yasgur. I've always liked him anyway but the fact that he did this, despite all the flack I know he got from certain members of our community (ahem, Dad). And then, on top of that, what he had to say about it all. It's pretty inspiring.

Ned walks back into the tent then—he stepped outside to hear the speech better—and he catches me smiling. He quickly smiles back. I let our eyes meet for a moment, acknowledging Mr. Yasgur's beautiful words more than anything, and then turn away.

A few minutes later, I can hear music start up again and I wonder who's on. Guess my human handbill is gone now.

A man comes in and announces that he forgot to bring his insulin shots. Anna tasks me with finding the correct syringe and tells me I can administer it.

I rummage in one of the bins and find it pretty quickly. Only then do I look over at the patient. Red hair and a pointy red beard. Not wearing anything except a small pair of underwear. I recognize him from somewhere.

And then I hear a faint *baaaa*.

On a hunch, I take a peek outside the tent. Sure enough, there's a sheep tied haphazardly to the post in front. Unbelievable. I'd bet anything that's one of Mr. Yasgur's flock, too. I'm about to go back in and give the dude a piece of my mind about animals not being playthings, when all words stop in my throat.

My mouth hangs open. All I can think is, *I have déjà vu.*

Approaching me are Evan and Rob, and they are carrying what looks like an unconscious Michael between them. The only thing different from the scene of two days ago is that this time the three girls lag right behind them.

I rush over to them. "What happened?" I ask Rob.

Evan points back with his thumb. "Him," he grumbles.

I look in the direction of his finger. To my surprise, I see someone holding a blood-soaked handkerchief to his nose. It's my brother.

"What?" I'm so confused. I go over to Wes to take a look at his face.

"He punched him," Rob says.

"Who punched you?" I ask Wes.

"No," Rob says. "He." He points at Wes. "Punched him." He points at Michael.

"Oh my God," I realize, horrified. "What?!"

"And then, of course," Evan continues calmly, "I had to defend my friend." He gestures to Wes's bloody nose. "Even though I'm a pacifist. Usually."

"Oh my God," I say again, lost for other words.

"I'm sorry, but he's an asshole, Cora," Wes starts, his voice nasal from the blood and the handkerchief. "Seriously, I need to start filtering your boyfriends. First, that guy, now this?" He nods at someone behind me and I stupidly look in that direction. Of course it's Ned, standing there frowning. We are, after all, not that far from the opening of the tent. I'm sure he heard every word.

"Are you out of your mind?" I seethe at Wes. "First of all, he's not my boyfriend." I realize I'm not sure if I'm talking about Ned or Michael. Both, I guess.

"You're damn right he isn't!" comes a voice from behind. I look to see Amanda storming up to me. "Can't we take him to another tent?" she asks Rob. "I don't want this hussy—"

"Hey!" Wes says. "Don't talk about my sister—"

"Oh, shut the hell up, Wes," I say. "I can fight my own battles. Thank you." And immediately, I'm struck with the thought of Amanda and me ending up with two broken noses ourselves.

But instead, I turn to her as calmly as I can. "Look, he's unconscious and he needs medical attention. Let them bring him inside. Now. Or do you want to risk his life because you're too worried he'll come crawling for me in his sleep?"

I hear Rob whistle under his breath.

I said I was calm, not that I wasn't feeling vicious. Also, I realize saying his life is at risk is a little dramatic. But then again, I don't think this girl can deal with anything other than drama.

"You stay away from him . . . ," Amanda sputters.

"Fine, whatever," I say, thinking quickly. Michael really

needs to get checked out, no matter who wants to claw out whose face. "I have other patients to deal with."

Of course, Ned is the closest person at hand, so, in my best brisk-nurse voice, I ask him if he can help the boys bring Michael in, and tell him that I'll be examining my brother.

Ned is silent as he leads the boys into the tent. The three girls follow. I'm sure they're going to get kicked out as soon as Anna realizes there's only one patient, so I need to make this quick.

I turn around and punch Wes in the arm.

"Ouch!" he says, dropping his bloody handkerchief to grab his arm.

"What the hell, Wes?"

"Look, he's with that pretty blond girl, okay? He's jerking you around." While he's talking, the medical side of me quickly starts to examine his face. I touch his nose lightly.

"Ow!" he yells again. "Stop it."

"I'm not trying to hurt you! I'm examining you," I say in exasperation. "Now, hold still."

His nose is definitely bruised but not broken. He breathes in through his mouth as I touch a particularly painful spot. "He's not jerking me around," I finally say. "I know he's with her. I've always known, okay? Besides, he's just a friend. Who's leaving town tomorrow," I add for emphasis.

Wes looks down at me. Neither of us knows what to say. I stop touching his face. "I can get you cleaned up," I say.

"Cora," he says. "I'm . . . sorry."

I sigh. "I know your intentions were honorable and all.

But is this really the time to finally find your courage?"

There's a beat where he doesn't know exactly how to react, until I smile up at him.

"Ouch," he says for the third time. "I guess I deserved that." He touches his nose gingerly. "What needs to happen here?"

"Not much we can do, really," I say. "The bleeding seems to have stopped. We can just clean off the blood."

"Okay if I run along instead then? That way I can catch some of the concert." He looks over at the tent. "And you can make sure your friend is okay."

I look at him. "Yeah, it's okay," I finally say. And then, right before he leaves, I have to ask. "Wait. Is this because you want Dad to see you finally got into a fight?"

He grins and shrugs before heading off.

I look after him and then take a deep breath before I walk back into the tent.

Sure enough, just as I expected, one of the other nurses is telling Michael's friends they have to leave.

"No!" Amanda says. "That's how we got separated for two days last time!" She sees me and glares.

"I'm sorry, there's just not enough room in here . . . ," the nurse continues.

I walk over to them. "What if you guys wait just right outside? He'll hopefully wake up soon. I'll come and give you updates. . . ."

"No way," Amanda says. "I do not need to see your bitch face ever again."

I stare at her. "Fine," I say in my most professional voice.

"He'll come give you updates." I point to Ned, who stands blinking at me behind his glasses. I can tell he's more confused than anyone as to what's going on.

"Now, if you'll excuse me, I have work to do." I see that my redheaded sheep friend is still patiently waiting for his insulin. I walk over to him purposefully.

As I give him his shot, Michael's friends file past me and out the flap. Rob touches my shoulder as he walks by. "Thanks, Cora," he says. I smile at him as I hold a piece of cotton to Sheep Guy's arm.

I'm bandaging up his arm when I hear my name again, this time in a weak voice.

I turn around. Michael is sitting up on his stretcher and smiling hazily at me.

Luckily, Amanda is already gone. I eye the flap warily and I make a point not to look at Ned, before I quickly walk over to the stretcher.

chapter 58
Michael

I don't know how I made this happen, but I know I'm grinning like a madman, even though it hurts my face. I'm back in Cora's medical tent and the back of her head is right in front of me. I'd recognize that raven-colored hair anywhere.

I call her name and sit up, much too fast as it turns out, because suddenly I feel very dizzy. I bring my hand up to my face and touch somewhere painful.

Cora's beside me in an instant.

"What happened?" I ask her, even though I don't really care. Somehow this beautiful, crazy festival brought us back together again.

"Well," Cora says, her big brown eyes just inches away from my face, "my brother punched you."

"Oh," I say, grinning again. Then, after a second, I think to ask, "Why?"

Cora takes a deep breath and goes to speak.

But she doesn't have to. I'm suddenly flooded with memories of this morning and my smile gets washed away with the deluge. "Wait. I know why. . . ."

Cora studies me. "Do you?"

"I'm an asshole," I say miserably.

"Why?" Cora asks, and she looks like she means it.

Is she going to make me explain it? I swallow. "Amanda," I begin. "And you. Look, I know I'm a jerk, but the thing is . . ."

Cora does the strangest thing. She smiles politely and puts her hand on my arm, as if to shush me. "Look, don't worry about it. It's my fault too. It's not like I didn't know you had a girlfriend." She shrugs. "Don't worry," she says again.

I look at her. I suppose that's meant to make me feel better, but it actually makes things hurt more. Like, internal things.

"But what if I want to worry about it?" I say, frowning.

"Why?" she asks warily.

"Because," I say. I touch her wrist lightly, remembering when it was sprouting feathers just a couple of days ago. Right here in this tent. "I like you. And this . . ." I stroke her skin. "It feels like something. Don't you think?" I look up into her eyes, willing her to feel the connection too. "I feel terrible," I say.

"You got punched in the eye," she replies.

"No." I shake my head emphatically. "I mean I've felt terrible all morning. Ever since you left last night, actually. And Amanda, I ended things with her."

Cora looks taken aback. "You did?"

"Well . . . ," I start out slowly, realizing that's not entirely accurate. "I was trying to before I got punched. I think she got the message, though."

Cora glances toward the tent entrance and mutters something that sounds like "I wouldn't be so sure about that."

"Well, then, I'll make sure she gets the message," I say emphatically, before taking hold of Cora's hand. I want to say this as right as I possibly can. It feels like the most important thing I've ever said. "It's you. These past couple of days, it's like everything's changed. *I've* changed. I can't stop thinking about you and I can't stop thinking about who I am when I'm with you. I like that person, Cora. That person is such a better man than I ever thought I could possibly be."

Cora sighs. "Look, Michael." It's not a good "Look, Michael." It's the type of "Look, Michael" I don't want to hear.

She extricates her hand from mine. "We had a nice day together," she starts. "A really nice day," she corrects herself. "But that's it. Tomorrow you drive back to . . . God, I actually don't even know what town you're from." The line between her eyebrows has appeared again and it's making me nervous.

After a pause, I realize she's waiting for me to tell her. "Somerville, Massachusetts," I say. "It's just north of Boston."

"Okay," she says. "You're going back to Somerville, Massachusetts. Just north of Boston. And I stay here. And that's it. Why kill yourself feeling guilty over that? Over one more day in Bethel, you know? What would be the point? Go back to your girlfriend and your life." She touches my face gently then, like she's trying to make it go down easier. "We'll just be a really nice memory."

I stare at her. The words hurt more than my eye, more than almost anything I've ever experienced. I touch the hand that's on my face. "But . . ."

There is movement behind her. Someone's at the flap of the tent, and Cora immediately gets up like she can sense it. A professional through and through. "Look, I have to get back to work," she says. She goes to a bin next to me and takes out two white pills. "Aspirin," she says. "I'd give you ice for your eye, but we're out."

"Cora . . . ," I start, but I don't even know how to finish that sentence.

Either way, she doesn't let me. "Look," she says again. I'm starting to hate that word. "Amanda's waiting for you outside. She's worried about you. And also . . . we really need the stretcher. Besides, someone is playing out there and you don't want to miss it, do you?"

I look at her, frustrated because there seems to be nothing I can say to make her listen to me. To make her understand.

"Who *is* playing, by the way?" she asks gently.

I listen carefully to the strains of music drifting through. "I think it's Joe Cocker," I finally say.

She smiles at me then, wholeheartedly. "I knew you would know," she says. She offers a hand to help me up.

I begrudgingly take it. At least it's an excuse to touch her one more time. She leads me to the exit, and I feel emboldened by the gravity of the situation. And by the fact that I knew it was Joe Cocker even after being punched unconscious.

"Wait," I say. "Can I just . . . can I get a good-bye kiss?"

Cora looks at me and the smile disappears. She sighs in frustration. I see her look around the tent at one of the older nurses who is busy with a patient. Then I see her stare at someone else. Only then do I realize that her ex has been here the whole time, the one with the glasses. He's pretending to be busy, but we can both see that he's glancing over our way every chance he gets.

Suddenly I'm angry. Sure, I'm going back to Somerville and I momentarily have a girlfriend, but what bullshit excuse does he have for letting her go in the first place?

Cora's looking back at me then. She leans over and I close my eyes out of habit. I plan to savor every moment of this. Only all I get is a brief touch on my cheek. A peck. My eyes fly open again.

"Good-bye, Michael," Cora says.

Her hand is on my back and for a moment, I think she's going to pull me in for a real kiss.

Instead, she uses it to firmly guide me right out of the tent.

chapter 59
Cora

I don't look outside to see Michael's reunion with Amanda. I just take a deep breath and try to gather myself. My face is warm and, I assume, flushed.

"Cora."

It's Ned. God, I am so sick of boys saying my name. I turn to him with a glare he doesn't entirely deserve. "Not now, Ned," I say, and sweep past him looking for something to busy myself with. Something medical.

He frowns but doesn't come after me. I tell Anna I'm ready for my next assignment, and she sends me over to an old man who needs his vitals checked.

When I say old, I mean it. He must at least be in his seventies if he's a day. I wonder what on earth he's doing here. His arms are bony and spotted and his back curves like a question mark in a white sleeveless shirt. But there's a spark in his eye that tells me he's at the festival by design.

He tells me his name is Ray.

"Was just having a little trouble breathing," he explains when I ask him how he's feeling.

I listen to his lungs.

"And how old are you?" I work in casually.

He looks at me and grins. "Why? Are you interested?" He laughs heartily at his own joke. "I'm just kidding. You're definitely young enough to be my granddaughter. How about we leave the age thing at that?"

"Okay by me," I say. "Any other medical history I should know about?"

Ray tells me he had a heart attack a few years ago and then tells me some of the medications he's on. I write it all down on his chart.

"I couldn't miss all this, though. Not the music," he says.

I stop and stare at him then, at this stranger six decades my senior who suddenly sounds so familiar, and I'm staggered by a rush of thoughts and memories that blow through me. Of Michael.

Just a few minutes ago, he was here, pouring his heart out to me, and I just brushed it aside. Told him we had a nice day, like it meant nothing more than that. Like *he* meant nothing more than that. When really, if I let myself think about how he said he felt around me, I felt exactly the same way. Like I was made of more than I thought but also lighter at the same time. And like someone believed in me.

Drops of water fall onto the chart I'm writing on. I'm crying.

Oh, no.

This is no good. No good at all. Crying for me is like showing anger. I don't do it very often but when I do . . . it's usually pretty epic. And uncontrollable. I can't even remember the last time I let myself cry in front of anybody.

The hiccups have already started, and Ray peers up at me.

"Are you okay?" he asks.

I mean to say yes but instead, I let out a huge wail.

I see Anna look at me in alarm and walk over. Out of nowhere, Ned has suddenly popped up at my other side.

In the meantime, the snot has started flowing freely from my nose and I am officially heaving. Loudly.

"Oh my God. Cora, are you okay?" Anna asks.

I make the mistake of trying to talk again, and bleat one more time. Then I make the mistake of trying to apologize for my bleat, with the undesired result of a loud honk. I shut my mouth and clasp my hands over it.

Anna has never seen me cry and she looks understandably horrified.

She takes the chart away from me and hands it to Ned. "Okay, you can't work like this right now. Let's start by breathing deeply."

I shake my head, not wanting to open my mouth again. My whole body is racked by sobs.

"Yes, you have to breathe," she says. "Here, put your head between your legs."

She helps me bend from the waist as I make gasping noises.

"Cora." I hear Ned's panicked voice and I shake my head violently. Funnily enough, he has never seen me cry before either. The night we broke up, only the hens were around for the result.

"Ned, please attend to the patient," blessed Anna says before turning back to me.

She strokes my back and gently helps me to stand tall again. She looks me in the eye with a small frown. "Cora," she says quietly. "I have to ask you. Did you take anything?"

I shake my head no before being racked by another hiccup.

"Okay, then what . . ." Anna looks at me and tilts her head. And in that moment, I think she understands. I suddenly appreciate that she was once a seventeen-year-old girl too. "You figured out what you want," she declares.

I take my hands slowly away from my mouth and open it cautiously, to make sure no strange noises escape. "I . . . think so." My voice comes out as a croak. "I think I have to go." I hear the scratching of Ned's pen stop. He's staring at me too.

"Of course you do," Anna says.

"I'm sorry to leave. I've been no help at all this weekend," I babble as I untie my candy striper apron. "I'm sorry."

Anna just smiles at me. "There'll be plenty for you to do at the hospital later."

Ned doesn't take his eyes off me as I leave the tent, but I barely notice. I feel a heady combination of foolish and giddy;

I feel invincible and simultaneously fit to burst with emotion, like I'm one pinprick away from becoming unbound.

Outside, I search in the immediate vicinity of the tent but Michael and his friends are gone. I head in the direction of the stage, knowing that I have to find him.

chapter 60
Michael

Joe Cocker's gritty voice is pouring sand into my wounded soul.

We're not too close to the stage; we're near the top of the hill, in fact. But the day is clear and I can see him pretty well, a thin man in striped blue pants roaring into the microphone with the most gorgeous primal scream I've ever heard.

I should be reveling in it. Instead, I'm thinking of everything that hurts, starting with my eye. Deserved pain, really. And it feels better than my insides right now, anyway, so I keep focusing on it.

Amanda has continued to pretend that we never started a conversation in the woods. She is talking excitedly about Cocker, how he's palpitating energy. How it's radiating up the hill and through all our fellow festivalgoers, who sway and twirl with him. She's right. But I can't feel it myself.

Everything looks duller. It might be my eye. But I doubt it.

Amanda loves Joe Cocker. She loves a lot of the same music I love. I used to think it was a miracle. And now it's starting to dawn on me that it doesn't really matter, does it? That just because we like some of the same things, or just because I think she's so beautiful, it's not enough to keep us together. Or it shouldn't be at any rate. Because that's not really what all these love songs, some of my very favorite ones, are actually about. They're about how someone makes you feel. Maybe, I'd even go so far as to say, they're about how someone makes you feel about yourself.

I have to finish what I started, even if it seems pointless. Even if I never see Cora again. I just can't keep up the charade of something, not when I've experienced the real version of it. It's disrespectful to everything I feel.

I move closer to Amanda and say her name softly. She pretends she doesn't hear me, continues to stare down at the stage in rapture.

"Amanda," I say again, more firmly. "Please. I need to talk to you."

She turns to me then, her gaze steady, her neck high, as if her perfect face is daring me to go through with it. "What is it, Michael?"

"What we were talking about before . . . before . . . you know." I gesture to my eye.

She continues to gaze at me, her expression blank. Does she really have no idea what I'm talking about? Do I have to start all over? I clear my throat. "I think, sometimes, two people aren't really meant to be together, you know?"

"Happier," she says slowly, out of nowhere.

"What?" I ask, bewildered.

"Before, you said we should be happier." So she does remember. "You meant happi*er*. As in, with other people," she says.

"Well, yeah . . . ," I say, though I don't think I like where this is going. Amanda is getting a black pinprick in the center of her eye. I recognize it; it comes along like the wick attached to dynamite.

"And by other people. You, of course, mean that bitch in the stripes."

"I . . . ," I falter. "No. I mean . . . Look, you and me . . ."

"You slept with her," she says matter-of-factly.

"What? No," I say. "I didn't."

"What did you do with her?" she asks, and her voice is calm. In fact, she is entirely still, like a cobra just about to strike.

Should I lie? I should lie. "I . . . nothing." But then I decide maybe I should do one honorable thing amid this shit fest. As my girlfriend, though soon to be ex, Amanda deserves the truth. It's not that bad compared to what she thought, is it? That we slept together. "We kissed," I finally say. "That's it."

Amanda doesn't move. She doesn't say a word. She looks me up and down slowly.

And then, an arm gets pulled back, and I feel a big blow to my shoulder. "You." Another blow. "Fucking." And another. "Cheater."

Soon she's flailing, her arm getting dangerously close to my busted eye.

I deserve the beating, so I just let her have at me, doing my best to keep my face out of her way. But then, suddenly, she stops. I look up, slightly afraid of what she could possibly have in store for me next.

But she's not looking at me. Her eyes are wide and they are staring somewhere right behind my back.

"YOU," she screams, and she's running up the hill behind me.

I turn around, confused until I see what she's running toward.

Cora.

chapter 61
Cora

I am frozen. Funny, because inside I feel like a thousand birds have just been released. I've found Michael and I saw the whole thing. He really and truly broke up with her. Even after what I said to him.

I want to laugh.

But then, I also have an extremely angry hundred-and-thirty-pound girl stalking toward me. The malice in her eyes is a force to be reckoned with. I don't think I've ever had something so deeply rage-filled directed at me before.

I take a deep breath and bring my arms up to my sides, ready to defend myself if it comes to blows. But before it gets to that, Rob grabs Amanda's arms and holds her back. She screams in frustration.

Michael is running up now and places himself between us. "She didn't do anything," he keeps saying over and over again.

"She didn't . . . seriously, Amanda. Stop it, please." Amanda continues to furiously struggle, trying to get out of Rob's grasp. "I'm not worth it," Michael continues. "You could get a million hotter guys. Right?"

"I CAN!" Amanda screams at him.

"I KNOW!" Michael yells back.

Amanda stares at him blankly. He's stumped her. Then she pulls her head back and spits in Michael's face before slumping down in Rob's arms.

"I'm done," she says. "I'm done. Let's go."

Rob looks at her suspiciously and then up at Michael, as if asking if he can let her go. Michael shrugs his consent.

Rob loosens his grip and Amanda doesn't look any of the guys in the eye. With her head held high, she glances at her two girlfriends. And together, almost as if it was planned, they forward-march down the hill and away.

One of them thinks to look back, probably realizing that Michael is their ride. But then, in a show of solidarity, she turns around and follows her blond leader.

Evan and Rob stand there watching them, not sure what to do.

Finally, Evan turns to Michael. "Er . . . so are we all driving back home together or what?" he asks.

Sometimes, you gotta love boys for their bluntness.

Michael laughs. "I'll meet you by the yellow medical tents. As soon as the concert's over."

Evan grins. "Cool, man."

He turns around to follow in the girls' wake. Rob walks

over to me, takes my hand, and kisses it. "It's been a pleasure," he says as he winks at me. He pats Michael on the back with a "Good one" and saunters away.

Michael and I are left alone. Well, as alone as we can be in a sea of four hundred thousand people. He smiles at me and I smile back. Neither of us says a word until Michael takes my hand.

"Come on," he says, and he pulls me up the hill and away from the stage.

"Where are we going?"

"I don't care," he says, practically skipping across the grass. "But everything seems brighter, doesn't it?"

Not really. In fact, some mighty dark and eerie clouds are rolling in and the wind has picked up, blowing flyaway hair all around my face. But I nod anyway. Michael's green eyes and his white teeth, they are all sparkling, like he's made of light.

"You were wrong back there, you know," I say as we walk, barely recognizing the airiness of my own voice.

"Probably," Michael admits, still with a full grin. "Though about what, specifically?"

I tug at his hand to stop him. "She can't do better than you."

His smile gets even wider and then, following my cue, he pulls me in and kisses me, slow and sweet.

"She can," he says when he finally pulls away. "And you definitely can. But I appreciate the ego boost."

"Well," I say, touching his chin lightly and scraping his peach fuzz with the tips of my fingers. "Maybe with someone who can grow a decent beard."

"Hey!" he yells.

I laugh and use my hand to direct his face back to mine.

I never knew how wonderful a little rough stubble could feel against my face.

chapter 62
Michael

The skies are not reflecting my feelings at all.

Joe Cocker killed it on "With a Little Help from My Friends," but it's almost like the intensity of his voice brought in the storm clouds.

The wind has picked up and is whipping our clothes and hair around us. When Cocker gets off the stage, an announcement is made to hold on tight as we sit out the rainstorm.

As if on cue, a huge rumble of thunder cracks the sky wide open and it is immediately pouring.

This isn't like the rain of Friday night, or the short sprinkle of yesterday. This is an honest-to-God deluge. We are soaked in moments.

Some people are trying to find things to go under, but most just follow the instructions of the announcements and stay where they are. A chant of "No rain" starts among the crowd and ripples out amid the claps of thunder.

I look down at Cora and I know exactly where I want to go. "Will you come with me?" I ask, taking her hand.

"Of course," she says. She doesn't ask where.

I lead her through mud and grass in a sort of high-knee march as our feet keep getting sucked into the wet ground.

I take her to the lake. I want my memory back. Or I want to create a new one, an even better one now that she's truly my girl.

The lake is almost completely empty, just beautiful symmetric ripples of water as the rain pounds into it. It almost looks like the water is falling up. It's perfect.

I try to lead us in, but Cora tugs my arm back. "Michael," she says gently. "Lightning storm. Electrocution?"

Oh. Right. I vaguely remember something about that from science class. That's why the lake is empty.

God damn it.

Cora squeezes my hand. It squelches with all the water that's between us. She smiles mischievously and then pulls me with her to an area by the side of the lake filled with short bushes and longer grass.

It feels like there is nobody there but us. The rain makes a curtain and I can't see anything except her face.

I want to kiss it everywhere. I start with the corner of her huge brown eyes. Then her forehead and the spot where the crease between her eyebrows sometimes appears. I kiss the top of her head and the start of her silky wet hair. I taste the rain-drops that are perched on her cheeks and chin.

Finally, I tilt up her face just a little so that I can get to her ripe, sweet mouth.

We kiss for minutes, hours, days. It's still not enough. Sheets of water fall around us; it's almost hard to tell where it ends and we begin. Our skin is slippery and soft, bursting the fat raindrops that stream down. It's like every nerve ending in my body has come alive and it tingles with every drop and every touch of Cora's skin.

Electrocution indeed.

chapter 63
Cora

I don't know if I'll ever be able to look at Filippini Pond the same way again.

I don't know if I'll ever be able to look at a thunderstorm the same way again.

Before Michael, all my previous make-out sessions have been semiprivate: in a car, or a barn, or a stolen corner of the hospital. I was never much for public displays of affection.

Now here I am, separated from half a million people by nothing more than a couple of scraggly bushes, and I find I don't care if anyone's looking. Maybe it's because we're also cloaked by the sheets of rain, and maybe it's because I know that almost everyone here is feeling some of the same magic that I am. It's in the air.

My lips are cold and numb and, eventually, one or the

other of us comes up for air. I take a good look at both of us, completely soaked and wildly happy. I grin.

Eventually, we leave our little cove by the lake and emerge to rejoin the rest of the world. The stage is still empty and the hill that leads down to the stage has become even muddier than before.

We watch a group of kids around our age huddle at the top and then one brave girl gets on her belly and launches herself down the muddy hill, screaming "Woooooooo!" all the way. She makes it about halfway down before her momentum gives out. Then she rolls on her back, muddy from her head to her toes, and laughs. She sits up and yells, "You have to try it!" to her friends.

One of them follows her advice and launches himself down too.

I can see people looking up at them, laughing, and starting to climb up the hill to give it a go themselves.

We watch the beautiful madness for a while, hand in hand, as everyone starts to become one color. No gender. No race. Just back to dirt and water and laughter. Who knew that the secret to happiness was hidden in the soil of my hometown?

"I almost bought you something," Michael leans down and whispers in my ear.

"Oh?" I ask, surprised.

He nods and then tells me about a vendor in the woods, describing a teardrop-shaped pendant to me. "It just reminded me of the lake and you in the water. The most beautiful image

I've ever seen. I didn't have enough cash, but I wanted to get it for you so badly. It was perfect."

I smile at him. "I love it," I say quietly.

"But I didn't buy it!" he protests.

"I don't care. I'll always wear it." I bend down and scoop up a dab of mud with my finger. Then I use it to draw a teardrop right over my sternum.

Michael grins and then bends down to get some mud of his own. In short, soft strokes, he finger-paints around my neck, creating a chain for my pendant. The cool mud mixes with his warm touch, and my skin drinks in a jolt that travels from my neck to my heart. I close my eyes, and only open them again when I feel Michael's lips softly touching mine. I look up at him, and then down at our creation, already washing away in the rain, and yet forever etched there in my mind's eye. "It's beautiful."

Michael touches his forehead to mine. "Aren't I just the most thoughtful boyfriend?" he teases. "Nothing's too good for my lady."

"The best," I laugh, surprised at how much him calling himself my boyfriend delights me.

We watch the mudsliders for a few moments more before my inner caretaker kicks in. "You must be hungry," I say to him.

He looks at me and shrugs. I take that as a yes.

I feel like there is only one place to take him. A part of me is scared to go there. A part of me is defiant.

But I take Michael's hand and start to walk away from the stage, away from Mr. Yasgur's farm, and to my house.

chapter 64
Michael

We walk hand in hand in the rain, past the grocery store and the fields and all the landmarks we passed just two days ago. When the world wasn't as promising as it seems now. Now I have the same person beside me but I belong next to her in a way I've never felt I belonged anywhere.

It's quiet when we get to Cora's big gray house, except for the persistent patter of rain.

She takes my hand and leads me straight to the front door this time. She opens it and I catch her looking around warily before she steps inside.

"Come in," she says. I can't help but look at the immaculate white tile that runs down her front hallway. I am dripping all over her front stoop and she is dripping all over the floor inside. I don't want to mess up her house. Not my first time as a guest in it.

"Cora?" A soft voice says, and I look to see the spitting image of her standing in the kitchen doorway. A little bit taller, and older of course, but the same dark hair and wide brown eyes. And, even, a smile for me.

"Could you get us some towels, Mom?" Cora asks.

She nods and disappears for a few minutes, emerging with two fluffy yellow towels.

"I'm Iris," she says as she hands me mine, and then proffers her hand.

"Oh, sorry, Mom," Cora says. "This is Michael."

I smile and take both the towel and Cora's mom's hand sheepishly. "Sorry I'm so wet."

"The clouds should be apologizing, no?" she says with a smile. "Are you here for the festival?"

"Yes, ma'am," I say, immediately slipping into my parental-politeness mode.

"How is it? Besides wet?" she asks.

"Wonderful," I say, and can't help but look at her daughter, who is using the towel to dry off her arms and face before wrapping it around herself.

I follow suit.

"Would you two like any food?" Cora's mom asks.

I smile. Apparently the resemblance goes deeper than just looks.

"That would be great, Mom," Cora says immediately. "We're starving."

"Come on in." She leads us into the kitchen and we sit down at a small breakfast table that's set up there.

"Dinner won't be ready for an hour or so still, but I can definitely tide you over with some leftovers in the meantime." She bustles around in the fridge and emerges with a few dishes covered in tinfoil. "You're not at the tent today?" she asks Cora.

"Not right now," Cora replies simply. Her mom doesn't press the issue further.

"Do you like chicken?" Cora's mom has turned to me.

"Love it," I say, and mean it.

She smiles and heads over to the stove to light it. "Did you travel far to get here, Michael?" she asks as she starts to heat up the food.

"Not too far. A couple hundred miles. I'm from just outside Boston. We've met some people who've traveled from much farther."

"I've lived here almost twenty-five years," she says. "Never seen anything like this."

"Did you go down there, Mom?" Cora asks.

"No, just saw on the television and the newspapers," she replies. "Dee went down yesterday and came and gave me a full report too."

"Dee is our neighbor," Cora explains to me.

Cora's mom asks a few more general questions about what we've been seeing at the festival. I keep my answers solely focused on the musical acts and not, say, on her daughter's body parts, even though that's all I'm thinking about.

Luckily, she doesn't probe too far.

Soon, I have a steaming plate of chicken, peas, and corn in

front of me. I dig in, only remembering about three quarters of the way through the meal that it's not entirely polite to completely inhale one's food.

The chicken is good, though not as good as my mom's. I actually surprise myself with that sentiment, but find myself thinking of her chicken cacciatore. With lemons and those little green, olive-y things. I forget what they're called. I seriously miss her food.

I admit, I even miss *her* a little. Despite the nagging.

That being said, when Cora's mom asks if I want seconds, I don't hesitate to say yes.

I'm just about to cut into my fresh helping of chicken when I hear the front door open behind me.

"It's an absolute disgrace out there, Iris," a man's voice grumbles. "I don't think even all this rain can wash away the stench of those hippies."

A squat man with a red cap walks into the kitchen and stops short as soon as he lays eyes on me.

"And who the hell are you?"

Out of the corner of my eye, I see Cora's face go gray.

chapter 65
Cora

I am mortified.

"Dad!" I cry at the same time that my mom says "Bernard!" in surprise.

Dad looks at me and we stare at each other, the air between us as taut as the wires in the chicken coop.

I collect myself and remember we have company. "Dad," I say, testing the waters like they're rigged up for electrocution. "This is Michael." I point over at him while mentally pleading with my dad to act normal.

Dad takes one look over at him, and then turns on his heel and walks out.

My mom gets up, addressing Michael. "I'm so sorry. Let me go see . . ."

But I stand up. "No, it's me," I say. I pull out my chair and place my napkin on the table. "I'll go."

Mom puts a hand on my arm then. "Cora," she says softly, looking into my eyes. "Please be nice. I know you can't see it, but his feelings run deeper than you know."

I suck in a breath and nod. Of course my mom would know what happened last night.

I find him in the first place I look. The barn. He's placed a bucket underneath April and is milking her.

I walk over before I lose all courage and change my mind. "Dad," I say softly.

He doesn't look at me.

I take a deep breath. "Look. I'm sorry. I was angry last night and I said some terrible things to you. I didn't mean it."

Silence, except for the distinct hiss of liquid squirting into the metal bucket. I wait.

"Didn't you?" he finally grunts, keeping his eyes focused on April's udder.

"No," I say. "I didn't. It's just, sometimes I feel like you treat me like a child."

"You are a child," he says.

"Not really," I say. "I'm seventeen. Next year, I'm going to college. I can't follow your every rule anymore, Dad. Some of them don't even make sense."

"College," he says with a snort. "I've always known you think you're so smart and I'm just an idiot without a high school diploma."

"I don't think that," I say, startled. "Not in the slightest. You've been running this farm since you were twenty, Dad. You've grown it. You've kept it profitable. And really, it's been an amazing place to grow up. I mean that."

I wait for him to say something, but he remains focused on milking, even though I can tell April's just about dry.

So I continue. "But it's the growing-up thing, Dad. You have to let me do it. Because the truth is, whether you allow me to or not, it's happening. Me and Wes. We're our own people now. You may not agree with everything we do or say, but I know you love us enough to let us make our own choices. Can't you accept you and Mom have already given us the tools to make good ones?"

Finally, he stops milking. He stares into the bucket for a long time before looking up at me.

"I'm not so sure we have," he finally says, his voice scratchy. "All that protesting that all those hippies do, that Wes does, that you agree with. You're protesting soldiers, you know. You're protesting Mark. And me."

I draw in a sharp breath. Is that what he really thinks? "We're not protesting you . . . ," I say softly, but it sounds weak even to my own ears. I never really considered this viewpoint before.

He shakes his head but doesn't say anything.

"Have you . . . ," I start. "Have you ever told Wes this?"

He laughs bitterly. "Your brother hasn't listened to a word I say in about a decade."

"That's because in some ways you're so different, Dad, but in some ways you are so much the same."

He gives April a pat. "You sound like your mom." He gets up then, taking the almost-full bucket with him.

"She's a smart lady," I say, trying to lighten the mood.

"Of course she is." He heads toward the barn's entrance, walking past me.

I touch him on the arm to stop him. "Dad. I *am* sorry." And I know that I'm not just talking about coming home after curfew or even cursing at him last night.

He searches my face for a moment before nodding. "Okay," he says simply. And I immediately reach over and hug him. He pats me awkwardly on the back.

"All right," he says. "It's over now. Let's not beat a dead horse, okay?"

"Dad!" I protest, feeling like a huge weight has been lifted. "Not in front of Shannon!" I point at our mare, who is glancing over disconcertingly.

"Shannon?" he says, shaking his head at the name. "Oh, girl. When will you ever learn?"

chapter 66

Michael

Cora's mother is the type of parent who doesn't feel the need to make awkward conversation with her daughter's friends.

I appreciate this about her.

After apologizing again for her husband (not necessary, I assure her), she asks me a few more questions about the festival, and then leaves me in comfortable silence while I finish the rest of my meal.

I insist on doing the dishes, though, and that's how Cora finds me when she comes back, with peach-colored gloves up to my elbows.

"Nice getup," Cora says.

"Does it bring out the salmon in my eyes?" I ask, batting my eyelashes at her.

"Definitely." She splashes some sudsy water at me. "The rain's letting up. You about ready to go back?"

"Definitely," I counter as I clean off the last fork and take off my gloves. I look down at Cora and grin at her, already feeling the excitement of the concert building in my belly. It's not over yet.

I glance around the kitchen to make sure we're alone, and then give her a quick kiss on the lips.

She looks a little embarrassed, seeing as her parents are probably only feet away, but she smiles.

As we head to the front door, I hear the click of a television being turned on in another room.

"Wait," Cora says. "Come with me."

She leads me to her living room, where her parents have just set themselves down in front of the TV. Even though there are two couches and an armchair, they sit right next to one another, their shoulders touching. I cannot remember ever seeing my parents that physically close to each other.

"Mom, Dad," she calls, and they look up. "My friend Michael and I are going back to the festival," she says slowly. "And I'd like to stay for the rest of the concert. But I don't know how late that'll be. Okay, Dad?"

He looks at her hopeful face for a second and then shocks the hell out of me by replying with a gruff "Fine, but be careful." Cora's mom gently squeezes his arm, and he turns his steely gaze over to me. "You too, Michael."

"Of course, sir," I immediately pipe up.

"Have fun," Cora's mom says with a smile.

"Thank you. Thanks. See you later." I can hear the relief in Cora's voice.

At the front door, she asks me to wait one more time, then disappears into the hall closet and reemerges with two thick red blankets.

"Wet ground," she says.

"Good thinking," I reply.

I take the blankets from her and hold them over my arms. Then we walk out of her house and make our way back to the glorious stage.

chapter 67
Cora

I know it killed my dad not to say what he was really thinking when he told me and Michael to "be careful"—i.e., "Don't do drugs." And probably—let's face it—"No touching."

But still, he didn't say I had to be back by a certain time. A+ to you, Dad.

The rain has slowed down but hasn't stopped by the time we make it back near the stage, and I have never seen more mud, or more muddy people, in my life. The impromptu mudslide is still going strong, but it actually looks like some people may have left during the storm. Now I can see even more of the piles of garbage that are dotting the brown landscape, everything from banana peels to toothbrushes to a bra.

In truth, Mr. Yasgur's farm is a huge mess, and it has me a little worried. Yeesh. Maybe Dad was a little bit right about how much of a disturbance this many people could cause on a farm.

But fewer people means we can get closer to the stage and Michael is thrilled. We sit down on our blankets and I can see everyone up close. Michael gives me information on each band as they come up.

First, it's Country Joe and the Fish. Joe looks like a pirate, with big hoop earrings and a wide patterned bandanna wrapped around his forehead. He's wearing a green army shirt, and he's hard to hear at first because they've turned the microphones off. But the rains stops sometime in the middle of his set and the sound system is back on in full force by the time he ends with a jaunty sing-along about ending the war in Vietnam. That's right after he leads us in a rousing cheer. "Give me an *F*. Give me a *U*. Give me a *C*. Give me a *K*. What's that spell?" He hollers and is answered with enthusiasm. I cheer along, but a little part of me is thinking about what my dad said too.

Then it's a band called Ten Years After, a shaggy-haired quartet that plays some long instrumentals with sporadic singing. ("Blues," Michael tells me.)

Then there's the Band.

We have a fun Abbott and Costello exchange there.

"This is the Band," Michael says.

"What band?" I ask, playing dumb.

Him: *The* Band.

Me: *The* band? As in, your favorite band? So emphasis on the 'the'?

Him: No, the Band. As in, that's their name.

I give a mischievous smile and he smiles back at me and

kisses my forehead. I lean back into him, glad I brought the thickest blanket since the ground is soaked. We listen to the band. Or the Band, oblivious to pretty much everyone until directly addressed.

"Hi there." I look up to see a guy in his early twenties with round glasses staring down at us. "My name is Greil. I write for the magazine *Rolling Stone*. Would you mind if I ask you some questions?"

"Um . . ." I look at Michael, who looks confused. "Sure."

"Can I have a seat?" Greil asks, pointing to a spot on the blanket.

"Yeah," I say, and scoot over.

He grabs a thin notebook and a pencil from his back pocket. "First, could you tell me your names and where you're from?"

"Michael Michaelson. Somerville, Massachusetts."

"I'm Cora Fletcher. I'm actually from here," I say. "Bethel."

"Really?" Greil says, looking interested. "So you live around here?"

"Less than a mile away," I reply.

The reporter then starts to ask me all sorts of questions about the farm and the town, what it looked like before, and how I feel about the festival being here.

"I feel like the circus came to town," I say truthfully. "It's wonderful."

When he goes on to start asking us about some of the things we've seen and done and our favorite acts, Michael finally interrupts him.

"I'm sorry. You said you write for *Rolling Stone* magazine?" he asks.

"That's right," Greil says.

"So you get to go to rock shows. And then write about it? And *get paid*?"

Greil chuckles. "Pretty much, yeah. Sounds like the life, right?"

"Sir, you will have to excuse my language, but fuck, yeah," Michael says.

Greil laughs. "That's basically the right attitude."

"How do you get into something like that?" Michael asks. His eyes are bright and he's suddenly sitting upright. If he had a tail, it would be wagging.

"Well," Greil says, "it's not easy. But then again, if you really have the passion for something, there's no way to stop you from getting to it, is there?" He looks at Michael thoughtfully for a minute.

"Tell you what," he says as he gets up. "I'm on deadline with this piece." He fumbles around in his pocket and emerges with a small rectangular card. "But this is my card. How about you give me a call sometime? If you're really interested in talking about it?"

Michael scrambles to his feet and takes the card. "Yes, sir. Thank you. Thank you so much." He shakes Greil's hand.

"Michael Michaelson, right?" he says. "I'll remember that. Sounds like I'll be hearing from you soon?"

"Oh, you bet," Michael says.

"Thanks to both of you for speaking to me," Greil says

pleasantly, before giving us a wave and sauntering off.

Michael slowly sinks down on the blanket again, staring at the business card like he can hardly believe it's real.

"Looks like somebody may have just found some direction," I say.

"Direction?" he says to me before pocketing the card. "I think that was my life calling."

Monday, August 18

chapter 68
Michael

It's past midnight when I ask Cora if I should roll out my sleeping bag. She nods her assent.

She lies down in it first, and then I arrange myself so that I'm curled around her, one arm over her waist. Neither of us says anything. My nose is in her thick dark hair. It smells like the sun.

Of course, then all I can think about is how much I must reek. Do lake baths really count? I didn't even use soap in the one I reluctantly had yesterday.

I move my nose closer to my own armpit and try to do a discreet body-odor check. But all I can really smell is the mud, which, as we know, doesn't smell too great to begin with.

Oh, well. Hopefully she'll just chalk up any foul smells to nature or whatnot.

I hug her tighter and she shifts into me.

The stars twinkle above us and I remember staring up at them just a few days ago, certain that they were divining something monumental for me. I thought it was just the rock festival. Now I know it's something infinitely greater.

I can't believe she can stay the whole time. I can't believe she's here with me. I find that more incredible than anything else I've seen all weekend. I wish the reporter were here now, because that's what I would tell him. That the best thing I've seen here is her, and it's going to continue to be her, no matter what Jimi's set is like.

The reporter. The *music reporter*. It's brilliant. I have to call him when I get home. Somehow, I have to make this work. And in a way I've never been sure of anything before, I know I will.

Sometime during Blood, Sweat & Tears's performance, I think both of us doze off. I'd never imagine sleeping during a rock concert, normally. But there's something about Cora's sun-scented hair, and the closeness of her body, and, I guess, just the fact that I need sleep at some point.

When I wake up, Crosby, Stills & Nash are on stage. It's too dark to see, but I hear the announcement and I recognize the song because I just got their debut album a couple of months ago. They're playing "Suite: Judy Blue Eyes."

I shift a little bit and Cora turns around to show she's awake too. She smiles at me.

"I like this song," she says softly. And then, as the guys sing about two people belonging to one another, she turns around so that we are face-to-face. She begins to softly kiss me.

The harmonies surround the length of our bodies, as they touch and move and shift. We never stop kissing. Not when she starts to undress me or I her under the cover of our sleeping bag, in the darkness of a star-speckled Bethel night. I don't overthink a thing. Not my inexperience or even my excitement. I let the music wash over me and give in to it, feeling that our bodies know everything they need to know and that nothing but beauty surrounds us.

I think we fall asleep with our lips touching. When I open my eyes again, the sky is bright with the risen sun and Cora is sitting up beside me, looking up at the stage. She has put on her clothes again but I am immediately hit with the unique sensation of open air whistling through my nether regions.

I search with my hands for my pants, which are balled up at the bottom of the sleeping bag, and then I do an ungraceful wiggle inside the bag to put them on.

Cora turns around to watch and laugh at me.

"Modesty looks interesting on you," she says.

"I'm sure you had to do the same thing to get yours on," I say.

"Nope. It was still dark," she says. "Well, ish." She shrugs with a sly little smile.

"I've created a monster," I say.

"Yeah, you and half a million other uninhibited people."

I sit up and kiss her shoulder. "I hope you don't decide to make streaking a regular hobby."

"I'm considering it," she says.

"What I meant to say is that I hope you don't decide to

make streaking a regular hobby unless I'm there to see it."

She grins and playfully sticks out her tongue.

I squint up at the stage to see who's on and am met with a bizarre sight. A group of guys in shiny gold suits are doing some sort of choreographed dance and singing an old fifties song.

"Sha Na Na?" I ask, confused. For some reason, I didn't know they were on the bill. Or maybe I saw it and my brain just disregarded the information since it made no sense.

But I look over and Cora is tapping her toes and mouthing along with the words.

I stare at her. "A favorite of yours?" I ask.

Cora looks at me and blushes a little. "We used to listen to a lot of these when we were kids," she says. "My older brother loved doo-wop and Elvis and all that stuff."

I smile. "Who didn't, huh?" I ask. "Did you have to sneak Elvis around your dad?"

Cora laughs. "Actually, I think my dad was cool with Elvis. Believe it or not."

"Elvis? The original rebel?" I ask incredulously.

"I know, right?" Cora says. "Maybe it has something to do with him being in the army."

"So this is not hippie music?" I ask.

She laughs, eyes wide. "Just wait until I tell Dad they played 'The Book of Love' here. It'll blow his mind."

"It'll trip him right out. Diabolical, Cora Fletcher."

She grins at me, and then unabashedly mouths along with most of the rest of Sha Na Na's set.

They get off the stage and I start to look around while they set up for the next act. It's really cleared out overnight. For the first time, I can see a lot more muddy ground than people.

When I look up at the stage, I know why I could never have left this show early.

There, at the very back, someone with a guitar is facing away from us. Someone with a telltale Afro wrapped with a pink scarf.

It's him. It's happening.

chapter 69
Cora

Michael goes into something like a trance as soon as Jimi Hendrix gets introduced. Jimi saunters out to the microphone, wearing a white fringed half-shirt with turquoise beading, his dark, flat stomach peeking through. There's a bright pink scarf around his forehead, and a gold hoop gleams from his ear.

"I see that we meet again," he says with an enigmatic smile before introducing his band. Someone from the audience yells out, "Are you high?"

"I am high, thank you," he says easily, and it's probably the most charming way anyone has ever made that declaration.

Then he plays. It's almost as fun watching Michael as it is watching the rock star. Michael's eyes are half closed and there are moments when he seems wholly intent on just Jimi's hands. I can see Michael's head move from side to side as Jimi moves his fingers up and down the guitar.

He told me Jimi was his favorite and I remember him getting all hyperbolic on me when describing his playing. I can see the fascination now.

There's an almost indescribable beauty about the man on the stage. Not just how he looks, but also what's happening up there between him and his guitar. His mouth hangs wide open as he plays, almost as if he has to suck in as much oxygen as he can to create that sort of energy. At one point, he starts to pick the strings with his teeth. The crowd goes wild and even I, who knows next to nothing about music, can tell I'm witnessing something special.

Michael and I hold hands but don't speak; I wouldn't want to ruin this moment for him. At one point, I recognize the melody that Jimi is picking out. It's "The Star-Spangled Banner" and I give a little laugh of recognition. Michael turns to me with a huge grin on his face, and then he pulls me close and places his chin on my head. We stay like that until Jimi stops playing.

Then there's a final announcement. They ask everyone if we can help with taking some garbage out as we leave, and thank us, and it's over. Time to go home.

Home. I am home. I can't believe it. The circus came to town and now it's leaving.

I look over at the boy still clutching my hand. Michael came to town and now he's leaving too.

When he looks back at me, my panic is echoed in his eyes.

We stand still as everyone starts to move around us.

Finally, Michael speaks. "I had an amazing time," he says, his voice a little hoarse.

I try to give him a big smile past the lump in my throat. "Of course you did," I say. "You just saw Jimi. You talked to Janis Joplin. You got mistaken for a rock god."

He shakes his head. "No," he says emphatically. "I had an amazing time. With you."

I take in a deep breath and then hug him. His voice reverberates at the top of my head. "I'm going to come back," he says. "I have to drive home now but then I'm going to come back."

Surprised, I break away from the hug to look up at his face.

"How . . . ," I start. But he doesn't let me finish.

He leans down and kisses me. It's not the kiss of a rock god this time. It's Michael's kiss and it feels as comfortable and right as the most sure thing I know about myself: that I belong working in a hospital.

It answers my question, too. I don't really need to know how or even when he's coming back right now. I just believe him. Someday soon, he'll be back.

We stay kissing and hugging for what seems like a long time as Mr. Yasgur's farm starts to finally empty out.

After a while, slowly, Michael rolls up his sleeping bag and repacks his backpack. I fold up the blankets. I know we're both taking our time.

"You're meeting your friends at the medical tents, right?" I finally say gently, when I know we can't keep putting off the inevitable for much longer.

He nods. "Walk me there?"

But I shake my head no. I think of Amanda and know that

I don't want my last memory of this weekend to be of her. "I think we should say our good-bye for now here."

"Our good-bye for now," Michael promises as he pulls on a strand of my hair and lets it slide through his fingers.

Then he suddenly dips me back to give me one final earth-shattering kiss. I swear I can hear Jimi's guitar solo start singing again in my ear.

Maybe there will always be a little bit of rock god in him after all.

chapter 70
Michael

It's strange to be going to the medical tents and be walking away from Cora instead of to her. She fills my every thought, though: her hair, her skin, the feel of her body. More than that, everything I've learned about her. Everything I have yet to learn.

I have a smile on my face when I think about that and all the time together that lies in our future. The time I'm going to find and make.

It's pretty easy to pick out Evan and the girls now that the crowd has thinned out so much. They're standing by the tents just like we said. Rob must have already split.

Evan gives me a hearty wave. Amanda scowls and looks away and, in a show of solidarity, Catherine and Suzie don't really look at me either. I don't pay much attention to any of it.

As we start to trek to the car, I ask Evan who his favorite act of yesterday was. He starts talking about Country Joe McDonald, when Suzie butts in and asks him how he could possibly say anyone other than Joe Cocker. A friendly argument ensues, one that Amanda can't help but get involved in too, and I'm happy that my question had the intended effect. I'm free to be alone in my romantic haze amid the noise of the conversation.

It takes us over an hour to make it to our car. We have to walk slowly down the emergency lane of Route 17B, partially because it has opened up again and there is traffic going by, and partially because we don't really remember exactly where the car is and have to keep a sharp eye out for it.

Finally we see it, the big purple boat gleaming in the sunlight. All that rain gave it a good car washing. My mom should be pleased.

We let out a collective shout of triumph as we run over to it, even Amanda.

But she refuses to sit in the front, giving Evan that honor.

As I start the car up and get ready to pull out, I think about the day that I can just turn around and come back here. To miraculous, wonderful Bethel.

I think I'll do it right after I sign up for a college course when I get back home. Maybe something to do with journalism. As soon as I do that, I can come back and Cora and I can spend the last weeks of summer together. For now.

But if this weekend has confirmed anything for me, it's how important now is. Now is all we have, really. And we never know when now will be the instant that changes everything.

So here's to keeping an eye out for that moment when some clueless executive mistakes you for Roger Daltrey.

And here's to fucking going with it.

Acknowledgments

Agents don't come any braver or truer than Victoria Marini. Thank you for helping Cora and Michael find the greatest home with the Simon & Schuster BFYR team. I'm especially grateful to Dani Young, for going to bat for a slacker hippie and a budding doctor, and doing so much to help them reach their full potential. Thank you times a million to Zareen Jaffery, for continuing that journey with me and for, quite simply, being a rock star of epic proportions. It's been such a privilege to work with you both. Thank you to Krista Vossen, for designing the cover of my psychedelic dreams, and to Katharine R. Wiencke, for copyediting with the precision of a guitar virtuoso. And thank you to Justin Chanda and the rest of the incredible team at Simon & Schuster BFYR. I have half a mind to organize and dedicate a three-day festival to all of you.

This book was my way to fulfill a lifelong dream and time travel to Woodstock. A huge thank-you to Wade Lawrence, director of the fabulous Woodstock museum at Bethel Woods Center for the Arts, who helped correct my poor grasp of geography and made sure that Cora and Michael inhabited the festival as it really was. (I also can't recommend a trip to Bethel Woods Center for the Arts enough—it's like your very own time machine.) Also thank you to J.P. McGuirk at Catskill

Regional Medical Center for answering some important hospital-related questions. Any historical inaccuracies are strictly my own.

I really do get by with ~~a little~~ a lot of help from my friends. This is by no means a complete list, but there have been writing-related e-mails, texts, tweets, and even good old-fashioned conversations that deserve my gratitude in print forevermore from: Katie Blackburn, Jenny Goldberg, Lizzie Foley, Chris Whittingham, Valeria Meniconzi, Dan Blackburn, Julie Henehan, Billy Henehan, Bryan Hall, Will Schneider, and Rachel Schneider. An extra-special shout-out to the inimitable Sarah Skilton, who has led by example on how to write fearlessly and stay both unflagging and gracious. Thank you still to the Apocalypsies and the Class of 2k12.

And, finally, a lifetime's worth of gratitude to my favorite Deadhead, my husband, Graig. Thank you for all your enthusiasm, patience, 1960s facts, endlessly explaining the concept of jamming to me, and casually coming up with crucial plot points (like the Roger Daltrey bit). Michael believes in Cora because you believe in me. I love you more than there are music and lyrics in the world.